FLYING TO YELLOW

FLYING TO YELLOW

Stories by

LINDA HOLEMAN

TURNSTONE PRESS

Turnstone Press
607-100 Arthur Street
Winnipeg, Manitoba
Canada R3B 1H3

Turnstone Press gratefully acknowledges the assistance of the Canada Council and the Manitoba Arts Council.

Some of these stories have appeared previously. "Flying to Yellow" was published in *NeWest Review*, "Lilyrose" in *Zygote*, and "Turning the Worm" in *Other Voices*.

Cover artwork: "Farmer's Daughter" (oil on canvas, 1938) by Prudence Heward appears with the permission of the Heward family. Collection of the Winnipeg Art Gallery; Gift from the Prudence Heward Estate (Accession #: G-51-170). Photo by Sheila Spence, Winnipeg Art Gallery.

Design: Manuela Dias

This book was printed and bound in Canada by Hignell Printing Limited for Turnstone Press.

Canadian Cataloguing in Publication Data
Holeman, Linda, 1949—
Flying to yellow
ISBN 0-88801-203-9
I. Title.
PS8565.06225F49 1996   C813'.54   C96-920015-3
PR9199.3.H6622F49 1996

for Jon

who helped me learn to fly

Acknowledgements

Thanks to the people who helped bring these stories together—especially Wayne Tefs, Catherine Hunter, and David Arnason. And thank you to Jamie, Manuela, and Christine, who made the production of this book a shared pleasure.

Table of Contents

Well, the world's open. And now through the windshield the sky begins to blush, as you did when your mother told you what it took to be a woman in this life.

—Rita Dove
"Exit" from *Mother Love*

FLYING TO YELLOW

RUM AND COKE. The odour, wafting from Myrna's glass, is making me feel queasy. Although it doesn't take much these days.

Rob and I sit shoulder to shoulder on the edge of a sagging brown plaid couch, in the small, stale front room of a cabin in a beach town on Lake Winnipeg. I surprised myself by saying yes when Myrna phoned to invite us, and didn't give Rob a choice, just told him we were going. Spending a July weekend with Myrna and Wally. I'll blame it on hormones when Rob and I unfold this sofa into a bed tonight and climb between the damp, worn sheets, and he looks at me and asks, in that low carrying rumble men use for a whisper, why I wanted to come.

I think I just wanted to share our news, face to face, with someone the baby is related to. I told all my family long distance, but I never got to see any of their faces, and I felt the need to connect with family.

Myrna is Rob's sister. She's forty-eight, only a decade older than us, but a generation apart. From the sketchy stories I forced out of Rob, Myrna just missed out on bra-burning, drug experimentation, free love, and hitchiking around the country. Instead, she spent her teen years stuffing her pointy bra with toilet paper, giving herself a home Toni and getting pregnant in the back seat of her boyfriend's souped-up Chevy.

At the age I was worrying about my karma evolving satisfactorily, hiding birth control pills from my mother and blotter acid from the cops at the Emerson border, Myrna was having three kids in four years, stretching a tight budget in a rented house in a run-down area of the city's west end. Her young husband worked for Grey Goose and drove across the windy silent prairies month after month, year after year, until one day he kept going, drove that silver bird all the way to Lake Louise and then walked away from it all, from the bus and the rented house and Myrna.

There was a second husband, one who came and went so quickly that Rob can't even remember his name. That was when Rob was studying at Simon Fraser, and pretty well lost touch with Myrna for awhile. Now Myrna has been married to Wally for six years, twice as long as us.

We sit here with them on this Saturday evening, in this cabin filled with musty paperbacks and decks of fifty cards and a Scrabble game with no letter S. It is their summer vacation.

"This is our first holiday together, since that weekend in Fargo after we got married," Myrna announces. "Sort of like a second honeymoon, eh, sweetie?"

Wally nods, then puts his bottle to his open mouth and tips back his head to let a long draught of Old Stock roll down his throat with a loud glugging.

"Wally rented the cabin from a friend of a friend, someone he knows from the Yards. Thought it would be nice for us to have a change, get out of the apartment this summer. Once we got here, I said to myself, well, I just have to invite Rob and Chris down. We don't see enough of you, Chris, you a career woman and all."

"You've always worked too, Myrna."

Myrna's laugh is throaty, rough, and followed by one short, barking cough. "Oh, I'm just a plain old working girl. Never tried to fool anybody into thinking my job was a career. No, just hard, honest work." She takes a mouthful of her drink, and in the middle of swallowing her eyes grow round and she flaps her hand at me. I sit forward with a mild tug of concern, thinking she is signalling that she is choking, but I relax back as she starts to speak again.

"Now Chris," she says, still waving her hand, erasing her words as they hang between us in the air, "don't you get me wrong. That didn't come out right at all. Of course your work is darn hard, and honest, too. People wouldn't trust lawyers if they weren't honest, would they?"

She leans towards me as she finishes her sentence, and the boozy smell of her breath makes my stomach roll. Everyone warned me about the mornings, but for me, evenings are the worst.

Myrna finishes her drink and, with an almost imperceptible nod, lets Wally know she wants another. He takes the Winnipeg Goldeyes tumbler from her hand and walks slowly and heavily to the little wooden counter that runs between the kitchen and the front room, hitching his pants up over his large belly. Squinting, he pours the dark rum into a glass measure, then dumps the contents of the jigger into the tumbler, adding cola to fill the glass. He drops in one ice cube, an afterthought.

Myrna's drink, rum. Myrna is true prairie stock—a stubborn, prickly perennial, regularly snowed under by life's woes, but always returning. Even after a particularly cold snap she will emerge, somehow smaller and less vibrant, but alive. A northern phoenix, nursing her Bacardi Superior.

After handing the drink to Myrna, Wally lifts his beer bottle with a flourish, and Rob and Myrna and I raise our glasses in an unspoken salute to something or someone, here's to ya, down the hatch. Maybe it's for me, to Rob and me, for the little seed unfolding inside me, or maybe it's to a good weekend, but nobody says anything. I glance at Rob, wait for him to speak. He always knows the right thing to say at just the right moment. Unless anyone asks about his family, his background. Or, obviously, if he's in the presence of Wally and Myrna.

Myrna takes a sip, and then nods at my glass of water. "I'm not supposed to be drinking, either. Not with the medication."

She brings the glass close to her mouth again, and stares down into its murky depths, studying the liquid as if waiting for a cue. When she looks up, she is smiling brightly. "But what the hey. You only live once." She sets the glass on the floor beside her, then slumps back in the burgundy crushed-velvet rocker, taking a final drag on her cigarette. She swivels to reach the ashtray on the arm of the couch, grinds the cigarette out with harsh jabs, then immediately lights another. She inhales deeply, shutting her eyes for a moment, the unexpected bright blue of her eye shadow startling in her colourless face. Then she opens her eyes and releases the smoke with a small satisfied sigh.

"Smoked for as long as I can remember," she says, looking at the glowing end of the cigarette. "I used to pinch Dad's all the time, remember, Rob?"

"I can't really remember, Myrna. I was pretty young."

"Sure you do. I used to get you to sneak them out of his pack." She chuckles. "He was a real agreeable little kid, do anything I told him."

I look at Rob, trying to imagine him running after Myrna, staring up at her with adoring eyes, but he is busy studying the TV guide. His face is a blank.

"Yeah, cigarettes got me through some tough times. No matter how broke I was, I could always scrape up enough for a pack of smokes."

She takes another pull on the cigarette, then touches it to the edge of the heavy glass ashtray with methodical, practised taps.

"Some mornings I don't think I could get through my shift if it weren't for knowing my break was coming up. Dreaming of a cigarette and a good strong cup of coffee."

Each time I talk to Myrna, she complains about having to work too hard, but I suspect she really likes the job. She's been at the same hotel coffee shop for thirteen years. Ernie, the chef, is her best friend; he's the only one on staff that's been there longer than her. When the manager isn't around Ernie will sometimes give Myrna a large foil pan of leftovers from a banquet. He also gave her a carton of Rothmans last Christmas, but Wally made her give it back. Wally eats the leftovers, but he draws the line at personal gifts.

"He's just jealous. You're jealous, aren't you Wally?" Myrna says, as she finishes the story about the Rothmans, her voice stretching out her husband's name, so it sounds like Wallllly. "Thinks old Ern has his eye on me, eh, Wally?"

Wally ignores her, leaning forward to stare at the small television. It sits on a wooden crate covered with a scrap of gold carpet, and is less than a foot from his black Naugahyde recliner. There is a rerun of *Bewitched* on, with the volume off. Myrna turns back to me, winking. "Specially when I wear something sexy to work." She stands, plucking at her pink cotton sweater.

"This is from Brad. You know, my middle one. None of my boys ever forgets my birthday."

I nod, reaching out to touch the nubby softness.

"I bet his girlfriend picked it out, and I bet it cost a bundle. He has this new girlfriend, Kelly. Brad says she always shops at those fancy little stores where they know her name. I guess they have lots of those kinda places in Toronto."

She strokes the sweater. It is crocheted, a summer sweater, and through the tiny holes of the needlework I can see her white bra. The scooped neck and short sleeves of the sweater expose her mottled, slightly puckered flesh. Her arms are long and hairless; her hands are long too, almost elegant, but their redness contrasts sharply with the white of her arms. She is wearing turquoise shorts, and her legs look as thin and brittle as her arms. Her midriff is strangely bloated for such a raw-boned, almost gaunt frame. Myrna pats the pastel pink roundness of her abdomen.

"I've gained some weight this month. Must be all the pills. Wally thinks it looks good. Wally likes a girl to have some meat on her bones, don't you, Wally?"

This time Wally looks at her and nods once, then abruptly sets his empty bottle on a woven green coaster, a misshapen water lily. Myrna watches him.

"Isn't it nice that Rob and Chris are starting a family, Wally?" She continues to caress her belly. "I've always loved babies. Some of those days when my own kids were tiny were the best times of all. Babies just bring out some happiness in a woman."

Her voice fades slightly, and she takes another long drink. Wally speaks. It's a rare event, Wally speaking.

"Didn't you want to talk to Chris about something, Myrna?"

I vaguely wonder if everything Myrna and Wally say to each other is in the form of a question, and for some reason, I can suddenly hear my heart beating. The cabin is far too hot, airless, the atmosphere heavy and expectant.

"Yes. Yes, I did," Myrna says. "It's about the operation. It's scheduled for right after my holidays."

The first I had heard about the cancer was earlier today. Rob told me in the car on the way down to the lake. I look at him now, but he has caught Wally's disease, and is staring at a mute, minuscule Darrin on the television. He seems mesmerized by the shrunken man's frantic attempts to escape from a teacup, while Samantha's scheming mother, I always forget her name, wickedly smiles down at him as she strokes a large drooling cat.

"Never mind them," Myrna says. "Men don't want to know nothing if it's got to do with a woman's"—her voice drops to a whisper—"a woman's business. Scares 'em, is what. Men are always scared of what they can't see right there in front of them. Let's go out, talk on the porch." She picks up her drink and cigarettes and matches, and, getting to her feet, nods at Wally and Rob. "I know Wally's dyin' to turn that set up, but I gave him what for yesterday, said when you folks are down I didn't want that thing blaring day and night so we can't have a decent talk. Don't know why there's a TV in a cabin anyway. Never heard of people watching TV at the beach."

I follow Myrna out to the screened-in porch. At least a hundred fishflies cling to the outside of the brown mesh, their wings swaying gently in the slight breeze.

"Look at those things. I won't turn on the light; they look worse in the light."

We sit in the darkness, and in a minute I hear the harsh rasp of a match. There is a brief flare of light, and then Myrna's ragged intake of breath.

"Shouldn't be smoking, I know. Doctor says there's a good chance this thing's already spreadin', something showing up on my lungs now, too. But it seems like I got enough on my plate; I ain't about to try and stop smoking on top of it all."

She stares out into the darkness, smoking. I wait.

"Now Chris, here's the thing. In case something should happen to me, you know, while they're operating, well, I'm real worried about Marcella."

The name catches me off guard.

Marcella.

"But isn't she still at the same place? She gets good care there, doesn't she? And the province covers the—"

Myrna doesn't let me finish. "Yeah, sure, all that's true. The nurses are good to her. I never seen her dirty or nothing. But there's no one else but me to really *care* about her, you know what I mean?"

I bring forward the one image I have of Marcella. It was a few days after Christmas, the year Rob and I were married, and we stopped off at Myrna's as we drove in from Calgary. We had spent Christmas with my family there, and Rob was feeling pretty mellow after all the attention my family showered on him. I was surprised when he suggested dropping in on Myrna and Wally; I had only met them

once, that October, just after Rob's transfer brought us to
Winnipeg. Rob never said much about them, just that we
had nothing in common.

When we drove up in front of their apartment block, we
saw Myrna leaning in the window of a cab that was parked
in the roundabout. We pulled up behind the cab and got
out. Myrna didn't hear us coming, and when Rob said,
"Merry Christmas, Myrna," she jerked her head out of the
window and turned around. Her eyes were red and wet, but
lit up when she saw us.

"Rob! And Chris! Hello, Merry Christmas." She
stepped away from the cab, pulling her parka closed and
folding her arms over her chest. "I was just saying good-bye
to Marcella. She was here for the day."

"Marcella?" I said, emphasizing the first syllable the
way Myrna had. Even though he was behind me, I could
sense Rob stiffen.

"Marcella, my girl. You can say hi to her. She won't talk
back or nothin', but she likes people to say hi to her."

I had never heard of Marcella. Rob's niece. He had
some old school pictures of his nephews. When we were
packing I found them stuffed in a shoebox. Each picture had
the date neatly printed on the back. A picture for each boy
for each year of elementary school, three times six.

Also in the box was a small, dog-eared photo album with
a couple of pages of black-and-white pictures of Rob and
Myrna and their mom. None of his dad, gone without a
word when Rob was ten or eleven. The black paper pages
were full of big empty spaces with dried-up bits of glue, like
someone had ripped the pictures off. In every photo Myrna
and Rob and their mother stand about six inches apart,
never with arms around each other, touching or even
smiling much, just looking at the photographer. That was
all I had of Rob's past—the album, and the envelope of
school pictures of three growing boys, mainly teeth and
ears. No pictures of a girl named Marcella.

I walked past Myrna and leaned down, smiling. The

smile stayed on my face as I looked at the person inside the cab. She could have been twelve or thirty. She was so huge that she spread out over the back seat, the buttonholes of her brown cloth coat straining at the edges. A plastic poinsettia was pinned to her collar, and her thin brown hair was held back from her forehead with a Minnie Mouse barrette. The thing I noticed, right after her immense body, was the small, odd shape of her head. Her face wasn't fat at all. It was almost delicate, with a neatly upturned nose and a pointed chin. Her skin was beautiful, very smooth and very white. Skin that could only be called alabaster.

"Hi, Marcella," I said. "Merry Christmas." She slowly turned towards me, and I saw that her eyes were a clear light blue, and totally empty. I didn't know whether she was blind, or just didn't see anything worth looking at. The opaque eyes stared at my shoulder, and I saw the faint shine of spittle on her chin. Her breath came in short gasping wheezes, and suddenly her lips opened in a sound, a choking grunt, and I stepped back before I could stop myself. Myrna touched my arm.

"She likes you, Chris. She's laughing. It's a big day for her. Christmas is about the only time she comes for a visit."

I turned away from the look on Myrna's face, my eyes meeting Rob's. He was pale, and he wore the same fixed smile that I had felt on my own mouth as I looked into the cab.

"Look, Myrna, we only had a few minutes. We can't stay," he said, with a forced little laugh. "Just tell Wally Merry Christmas for us."

"You can come up. We're not doing nothin'. Just watching TV. Come on up, I got lots of food."

The smile hadn't left Rob's face. "No, really, Myrna." He pushed back the soft suede of his sleeve and stared at his watch. "We're already late. We're going to dinner at some friends of Chris's."

I remember fumbling with my gloves, fixing each leather finger carefully in place as we said our good-byes.

We followed the cab away from the apartment, trailing it until it turned in the direction of the river.

As we passed the twinkling trees and wreaths that lined the main boulevards of downtown Winnipeg, Rob told me that Marcella had been born between Myrna's first and second husbands. The father left the city before Myrna even knew she was pregnant.

Myrna had tried to look after Marcella herself, Rob said, but the little girl had too many problems. Doctors convinced Myrna that putting Marcella into an institution would be best for everyone.

"But why didn't you tell me about it before?" I asked him, after he had fallen silent.

Rob shrugged, and didn't answer until he eased the car into the garage and turned off the engine. He sat with his hands on the wheel for a moment, then said to them, "Look, Chris, it's easy for you to talk about your family. Everything's right there, hanging out for anyone to see. Everyone knows all the little details about the last six generations. A family tree would definitely not be a good idea with my lineage. Too much transplanting and grafting, not enough roots, if you know what I mean. You're just going to have to understand that there are some things I'd rather not talk about. I worked too hard to get away from the life I was born into, and make the one I have now. Drop it, O.K.?" He lifted his hands and brought them down once, hard, on the wheel.

I dropped it, and so it caught me off guard tonight when I heard Marcella's name again after all this time.

Myrna waves her cigarette in the direction of the screen. "Funny thing, them fishflies. Seems like maybe they can see colours, but I don't know for a fact. Early this morning I took myself out for a walk, along the road. It was beautiful, so quiet. I looked at all the other cabins, just wondering about the people inside, who was sleeping, who was up making coffee, and darned if I didn't notice that those fishflies were covering the cabins painted yellow. Every cabin had their share, but those yellow ones, well, you could hardly see the wood at all for their bodies, just hanging there, all tremblin', like they was waiting for something."

Filling her lungs, she holds the smoke for a long time before blowing it out and continuing.

"Or maybe not waiting at all. Maybe just enjoying the yellow. I thought to myself, funny how a thing so mindless can still figure certain things. Flying towards whatever it is that makes 'em happy."

I take a sip of my water. "I guess it's just instinct, Myrna. Gravitating towards something that you know feels right."

There's a minute's silence in the little porch. "Well, I don't know much about instinct and gravity," Myrna says. "All my life I just did what I had to do, on my own, mostly, and had my share of happy times. I never expected nothing and never got nothing for free. Never asked no favours. But I got a favour to ask now, Chris. You can say no, I'll understand, but I gotta ask."

I nod, not sure if she notices.

"It's about Marcella. Like I said, you can say no." Myrna's voice is slower, softer than usual. "It's just that there's no one else. None of the boys live here anymore, and besides, they all have their own lives. And Wally"—her voice drops still another tone—"he means well, Wally does, but he'd be no good at the kind of thing I'm talking about." She leans forward, the old wicker rocker shrieking. "What it is, Chris, is if somethin' happens to me, you know, because of this cancer, and the operation and all, I just keep thinkin' about Marcella, and the holidays. I don't see her regular through the year, the bus don't run there and it's too expensive to take cabs and Wally wants me home on the weekends. But the special times, like Christmas, and her birthday, maybe Easter, well, I know she knows somethin', Chris. The nurses tell me, they say those eyes start focussing and she keeps getting out of bed all night right before I visit.

They say she stares at that door and they can't tear her away, not even for meals, for a few days before I'm coming. I always tell her, see, always show her the calendar and promise that I'll be there. Course she doesn't know about weeks or months, but the nurses say she knows something's up, knows something's gonna happen. And then I think if suddenly I don't show up anymore, and she never gets a visitor, not ever, well . . ." The rocker creaks back and forth. "Marcella's surprised everyone by staying alive so long. Her heart's no good, you know. But she's happy where she is. It's the only place she knows."

I visualize the old brick house with wire over the windows. I'd seen it from the river when Rob canoed down the Red with me our first summer in Winnipeg. He was trying to convince me that the transfer hadn't been a mistake, that his flat boyhood city could be pretty once winter was over.

Although the tall narrow building was nondescript, the grass that ran down to the river was green and soft, and the circular flower beds near the back of the house were colourful and well tended, surrounded by wooden benches. In the middle of one of the beds was a purple martin birdhouse.

"What's that place?" I had asked, pointing.

Rob threw a glance in the direction of my finger. "An institution. For disabled people." The paddle dipped almost soundlessly into the smooth surface of the water. "Marcella lives there."

"Have you ever been inside?"

"Nope." Rob turned back to face the bow, the muscles in his bare back stretching and releasing as we pulled away from the broad expanse of green on the riverbank beside us. His usual controlled strokes now held an awkward touch of panic, as if by his acknowledgement of the place invisible fingers might suddenly reach out to touch him.

"Chris?" Myrna's voice brings me back to the porch. "I'm not asking you to do anything special. She don't need anything; all her clothes, medicine, whatever, is supplied. It's just to, well, drop in on her, once, maybe twice a year. I always take her Liquorice Allsorts, they're her favourite, even though the nurses don't like her having sweets. Upsets her system, and she don't need the calories, that's for sure. But it does make her laugh, to see those Allsorts. She spreads them out in her lap and picks 'em over real careful, touching each one. She especially likes the ones that look like little jewels, all covered in tiny beads, blue or pink. She touches those the most."

I reach out to the screen and press my finger against a fishfly, exerting soft pressure against the still body. It doesn't move.

"It's just that I'd like to go under knowing. I can't get it out of my head that I might not come out of it, you know? And Marcella is sort of like, well, like unfinished business. I want to know that there would be someone here to . . . care about her. I know you're not real family, not blood, like, but you're the only one I feel I can ask. It seems women just understand these things. Especially mothers."

I put my hand on the swell between my hips, aware that Myrna is watching me.

"Rob says you'll be a real good mother, Chris. He says you got a big soft spot, but you won't take no nonsense. Says you must be understanding to put up with him. That's why he said I should go ahead and ask you. About Marcella."

"You've talked to Rob already?" With the door of the front room behind her, the dull light from the television turns Myrna's platinum perm into a wiry blue nimbus. Beyond her head, I see part of Rob's face, the clean line of his jaw, the curve of his lips.

"I talk to him a lot. Phone him at work, when I got a problem."

I watch Myrna's fingers lace and unlace in her lap as I try to visualize Rob talking to her from his polished mahogany desk, high above the city.

"So when I told him what I wanted to talk to you about, he said I should go ahead, that he knew what you'd say, but he couldn't say it for you."

She stops, suddenly, and I look up at her.

With the light behind her, her features are planed smooth, sharp edges melted. It's an unlined face, the face of the girl in one of the black-and-white photographs. She stands stiffly beside her little brother, and she holds a small white dog against her chest. Her chin is held high, grazing the fluff on the top of the puppy's head, and she stares into the camera, boldly, but her eyes betray her.

A sudden wind rustles the poplars and aspens that surround the cabin, and with a whisper of transparent wings, the fishflies rise as one and leave the screen, letting the cool fragrant air from the lake wash over us.

AT A LOSS

AFTER THEY HAD MOVED HER from Emergency into a room, Lyle went home to gather up some of the mess off the bathroom floor. The blood containing tissue. Janine thought about the look on Lyle's face when they asked him if he could retrieve a sample for them, how it could help in their diagnosis. He hadn't looked at her, just nodded, quickly and agreeably, as if it were a common request.

Take the spatula, Janine had wanted to say. Scoop it up with the old spatula you keep with your tools, then carefully slide it into a clean ziplock bag. Don't use the empty jar under the sink; it had artichoke hearts in it, and I only rinsed it for the recycling bin. There's still grease and tiny oily particles on the sides of the jar. If you put the stuff that came out of me in there, it may confuse the issue, they may not be able to run proper tests.

She wanted to tell Lyle all that, but when she opened her mouth, the index finger on her right hand moved up and down, up and down. No words came.

Eventually the bustle surrounding her stopped, and she was alone. She slowly moved onto her side, cradling her arms over her abdomen. She knew it wasn't empty yet, not totally. The intern on duty had explained to Lyle about the need for a D and C.

She tried not to imagine the scraping, the pulling at her uterus, the sharp instrument ripping off the last microscopic cells, cells that were already growing into a dimpled starfish hand, the delicate spiral of a cochlea. She hugged the slight bulge of her belly more tightly, wanting to comfort any part of her child that had refused to go willingly, still clinging to the walls that had been its home for over twelve weeks.

The intern in Emergency had been young and tired. He stood back as the nurse snapped on her gloves and pushed Janine's knees apart, pulling away the tightly wedged hand towel, now crimson. Janine had covered her eyes with her arm as the intern examined her, letting Lyle answer the questions. When did the cramping start? How long had she been bleeding? Had she fallen? Had a shock? Been ill? How old is she? How many pregnancies? Has she miscarried in the past?

When he was done, Janine uncovered her eyes. The intern was scribbling on his chart, but unexpectedly he glanced at her. She was suddenly aware of her limp hair, streaked with grey, the darkened pouches under her eyes, the ragged Grateful Dead sweatshirt she had thrown on, intending to give the kitchen cupboards a good going-over.

"The physical examination doesn't give any indication for the spontaneous abortion, Mrs. Coghlin." The words were technical, but the voice kind. Personal, with a hint of weary regret. "If the tissue Mr. Coghlin brings back doesn't show us anything, we may have to assume there is no real cause, as is the case in so many miscarriages. Or . . ." He looked down at the chart, back to her face. "It could be your age. At thirty-nine, the body doesn't always adjust to the pregnant state as easily as it does in a younger woman."

I failed because I am too old, Janine thought; there is no suitable reply, no argument. For one of the only times in my life, I am at a loss for words.

Janine visualized her mouth, opening and closing, soundless.

I have even lost my words.

To her horror, she felt a sudden grin tugging at the corners of her lips, a hysterical reaction similar to the helpless giggle that sometimes slipped out at shocking news. She covered her mouth with her hand.

Misunderstanding the gesture, the intern tried to make amends. "You can certainly try again; there doesn't appear to be any physical damage, and your medical history is good. But to be safe it's important that you wait for three complete cycles before attempting to conceive."

Janine listened to the textbook words, watching his face. The lower lip, full and sensuous, a bit like Lyle's. Her colouring, fair hair and dark eyes. Perhaps her baby would have looked like this handsome young doctor.

"Mrs. Coghlin?"

Janine forced her gaze away from his lips, and opened her mouth, but again, only her index finger moved up and down.

"I'm sorry, Mrs. Coghlin. Perhaps this isn't a good time to discuss this." He looked at Lyle.

Lyle cleared his throat, rocked back and forth ever so slightly.

"We'll keep your wife in overnight, Mr. Coghlin, do the D and C first thing tomorrow morning. She should be ready to go home later in the afternoon."

Janine wondered why Lyle didn't tell the intern that he wasn't Mr. Coghlin. That they weren't Mr. and Mrs. anything. She waited for Lyle to set the record straight, but instead he held out his hand. The intern looked down at Lyle's outstretched hand, green paint rimmed around the nails, then shook it.

"Alright then, Mr. Coghlin, we'll get your wife settled and you can come up to see her tonight."

As he wrote one more thing on the chart, Janine noticed a thin line of perspiration on his upper lip. Maybe his first miscarriage too. As he left, Janine imagined relief in the sag of his shoulders.

Lyle came over to her, his face vague, distant, hiding something. Sorrow, or disgust at what he had to do now, or, like the intern, simply relief?

Janine couldn't tell. Lyle kissed her forehead, then patted her arm. The pat you give an old woman when she's upset over some trivial misunderstanding, some slip of memory. There, there, the pat said. There now, don't worry about it.

Lyle brought Donovan to see her that evening.

"Hi Mom," Donovan said, standing at the foot of the bed, studying the bumps of Janine's feet under the thin blanket.

Janine gave him a little wave. She didn't even bother to open her mouth. Waiting for the afternoon to pass, dry-eyed and alone in the cheerless room with its humming fluorescent light, she had tried to talk. No sound would come out, but her finger would start its ridiculous wagging. Janine wouldn't look at her hand, but she could feel the finger working away.

Donovan turned the hoop in his left ear. He shrugged, then a few seconds later, shrugged again, as if carrying on an internal conversation.

"So. Lyle says you're gonna be O.K. He says you can come home tomorrow."

Janine nodded, and Donovan fumbled in his jacket pocket. He held out a Mr. Big. "It was too late to get you anything, you know, flowers or anything, so I picked this up at the 7-Eleven."

She took it, smiling at him.

He looked at the smile, then shrugged again. "Sorry."

Sorry for the chocolate bar, sorry for never wanting her to have a baby, sorry for being glad it was gone? Janine was tired of trying to understand the expressions and gestures. She always thought of herself as intuitive, reading the little nuances clearly. She blamed the sudden dysfunction on the large earthy clump that was lodged somewhere between her mouth and her chest. The dry chunk made it hard to make sense of things, made it hurt to swallow and breathe, impossible to speak. She wanted it to move, to shift one way or another. She wanted to spit, to force it out in a foul rush into the aluminum kidney dish sitting on the scratched bedside table. Or swallow, deeply, push it down into the maze of organs, where her stomach acids could dissolve it into a benign substance to pass through her intestines. But she had no saliva, could only manage small, tight swallows.

"I think I'll go grab a cup of coffee," Lyle said. "There's a machine on the next floor. Do you want me to bring you something, Janine? Juice, or tea?"

She shook her head.

When Lyle left, Donovan pulled the straight chair from against the wall up beside her. He glanced at the empty bed under the window.

"At least you've got the room to yourself. Better than having to share." As soon as he said it, Janine saw a faint flush wash over his face. He started running the zipper of his jacket up and down, zipping and unzipping, as if trying to rub out what he'd said.

Janine wanted to tell him she understood, wanted to console him, tell him she knew how he meant it. Just a simple statement, something to say. No offence intended, none taken.

She thought of his room at home, the small crowded second bedroom in the ground-floor apartment of a house. The huge old house, divided into separate suites, sat between other formerly elegant houses in an area that could be trendy in a few years. Now it was just shabby, the rent cheap.

When Janine had told Donovan about the baby, six weeks ago, he was furious.

"You're pregnant?" He studied her face to see if there was a joke coming, but then his voice became indignant, breaking briefly in the adolescent squawk that still surfaced occasionally. "You're friggin' pregnant? Jeez, why'd you have to go and do that?"

"It just happened, Donovan," Janine said, patiently, slowly, as if explaining how she'd lost her keys or forgotten to wash his jeans when she knew he needed them. "I never dreamed I'd get pregnant. Especially not now. You know I wasn't ever supposed to be able to. You were a total shock, but the best thing that ever happened to me. You know that, honey." She reached up to touch his cheek, noticing the tiny glint of new gold along his jaw line. He brushed her hand aside.

"Yeah, but that was different. You and Dad were married, you said you had something going. But you and Lyle. Jeez. And your work." He didn't say "and me," but Janine heard it. "A baby will just screw everything up."

"What will it screw up?"

"Only our *lives*, Mom. It'll screw up our lives."

Janine didn't say anything; she didn't tell him that Lyle's reaction hadn't been any more enthusiastic than his, although slightly more mature. Lyle was a nice man. He had a lot of good qualities. He also had two children, and had told her, shortly after they met, that losing them had been the biggest sorrow in his life. He didn't ever want to go through that again. They lived with their mother down in Colorado, and he hadn't seen them in three years. Janine knew he always met his child-support payments, and in the two years they'd been together, he'd never missed a birthday or Christmas gift and phone call.

"Do you really want it, Janine?" was all he said.

"Yes. I definitely want it." Her hands hovered protectively in front of her. "But it's mine, this baby. You don't have to do anything, or take any responsibility. I won't even put your name on the birth certificate."

And it had been hers, but too briefly to start any of the usual preparations—thinking about names, buying tiny undershirts and sleepers, signing up for a Lamaze class, investigating daycare. The only thing Janine had done was buy a bassinet. A week after she had told Donovan about the baby, she'd seen the bassinet at a yard sale a few streets over from her apartment. She'd driven by, then stopped and backed up.

The bassinet was in good shape, the white wicker clean and unbroken, the eyelet skirting covering the legs stiffly ironed. A piece of masking tape on one side displayed a large $15.00.

"It looks so new," she said to the young woman sitting on a lawn chair. The woman threw a Tupperware celery keeper into a big cardboard box near the chair.

"Yeah. I got it as a gift from my in-laws, but I hardly used it. They're only good for six weeks, two months at the most. By then the kid's getting too big, time for a crib. I wish they would have given me something practical, a car seat or a high chair."

Janine's smile indicated that she knew all about the problems of in-laws. "I only have $10.00," she said. "Will you take $10.00?"

The woman stood up. "Sure. It's been sitting here all day, and no one's even looked at it. I don't want to have to haul it back to the attic." She took the two fives Janine held out, looking more closely at her.

"So who's it for?" she asked.

Janine finished putting her empty wallet back in her shirt pocket, aware of the slight pressure against her tender breasts. She was offended by the woman's tone, curiously afraid of her reaction.

"It's just a present," she said. "A present for a baby."

There was no room for the bassinet in the bedroom where she and Lyle slept. Until she felt the time was right to ask Lyle to start moving furniture around, she put the little cot in Donovan's closet. Although his was the smaller of the two bedrooms, his closet was much deeper and longer. It had rows of drawers with fancy brass pulls on one end, and a glass-doored cabinet at the other. Instead of the usual closet fare, a bare bulb with a string, it had a frosted-glass fixture with a long chain ending in an ancient frayed tassel. Janine was sure the closet had been a butler's pantry; the kitchen was on the other side of the closet.

She pushed the bassinet in front of the empty cabinet, and covered it with an old sheet.

Watching Donovan pulling at his jacket zipper, Janine remembered his reaction to the draped bassinet in his closet. He said it wasn't fair; he'd always had his own room, and this was not the time to start having to share his space.

He was right about always having his own room. Even after the divorce, when all Janine could afford was a one-bedroom apartment, she'd given Donovan the bedroom. She slept on a rollaway in the tiny curtained alcove off the kitchen, described in the newspaper ad as a "dining nook." Waking up cramped and weary after her nights on the narrow bed, she would tiptoe to Donovan's room, surveying the scattering of Lego and Mr. Potato Head pieces around the double mattress on the floor. Donovan would be stretched out, hugging his "sleepy," a stuffed Snoopy with an unnaturally large head and a pair of felt Red Baron glasses stitched around black, expressionless eyes. Seeing her son sleeping so contentedly, surrounded by all his favourite things, she felt less guilty about taking him away from everything he had ever known.

In the loud silence of the hospital room, she picked up
Donovan's hand and squeezed it, hard. A nurse came in at
that moment, heavy thighs rubbing against her pink nylon
uniform. Donovan snatched away his hand and stood up.

"Don't worry about me," the nurse announced
cheerfully. "Just here to take Mrs. Coghlin's temperature,
check her pulse. You don't have to leave." She reached over
Janine's head for the black velcro armband hanging from a
hook on the wall.

"It's O.K. I was just going. I'll find Lyle." Donovan
stood over her for a moment, watching as the nurse
wrapped the blood-pressure band around Janine's upper
arm.

"I'll see you tomorrow, Mom." All of a sudden he
leaned down and kissed Janine's cheek, then hurried out of
the room. At the unexpected touch of his lips, Janine felt a
tiny painful prick at the back of her eyeballs, and the
boulder crushing her larynx gave a lurch. Janine opened her
mouth, tentatively.

"Thank you, dear," the nurse said, popping in the
thermometer.

Early the next afternoon Janine stood beside Lyle as he
talked to the doctor at the desk, then she took the pen and
obediently wrote her name on the lines Lyle pointed to. She
put her hands back in her pockets. She wanted something to
carry; everything felt empty, her hands, her arms, her body.
Only her throat was full, the pressure of the lump pushing
painfully on her Adam's apple.

She waited at the hospital door while Lyle brought the
car from the parking lot, then carefully slid in, leaning her
head back against the seat and shutting her eyes.

"You O.K., Jannie?" Lyle asked.

Janine kept her eyes closed, nodding. As a toot sounded

from the car behind them, Lyle started away from the hospital. He immediately switched on the radio and turned up the volume, louder than she knew he liked it. She kept her head away from him, looking out the window at the panhandlers on Market, then at the leaves piled into small crunchy pyramids on the boulevards, and finally at the cracked, uneven sidewalk in front of her own place.

As she got out of the car, Lyle came up beside her and put his arm around her shoulders. He opened the front door for her, then unlocked the door to their apartment and stood back for her to pass in front of him into the tiny foyer. Janine felt a stab of unexplained fear, hesitated at the doorway before stepping in. As she hung up her jacket, Lyle went into the kitchen, talking over his shoulder.

"Why don't you go and lie down for awhile, Janine? I'll make some coffee. Donovan has basketball practice after school, and won't be home until about five. I picked up some lasagna for supper."

Walking slowly down the hall toward their bedroom, Janine kept her eyes fixed straight ahead. She didn't want to look into the bathroom. She knew it would be washed clean, but she still didn't want to look.

She started to pass Donovan's room, but stopped at the door, holding on to the frame. Then, stepping over the clothes and magazines in a few strides, she opened the closet door and pulled the ragged tassel hanging from the light bulb.

Janine knelt down by the covered shape against the cabinet. She touched the sheet, then abruptly pulled it away. Staring into the tiny white bed, she looked at the stuffed dog she hadn't seen for at least eight years, the one she always thought had been lost in one of their many moves. She picked it up, brought it to her face and breathed deeply. She touched the torn ear, noticed the red goggles were gone, and fingered the awkward bow of the new yellow ribbon tied around the dog's neck.

Without warning she began choking, a retching, ugly

noise. She pushed the closet door shut and balled the sheet up against her face. She rocked back and forth on her knees, deadening the horrible keening with the sheet, Snoopy trapped against her chest.

When she was finally limp and silent again, she put the dog back into the bassinet, smoothing the wrinkles out of the ribbon with her fingers. Then she wiped her face with a dry corner of the sheet, shook it out and spread it back over the bassinet, the way she'd found it.

She opened the closet door and smelled coffee, the expensive blend of Irish and Swiss Mocha she usually couldn't afford.

"Janine? Jan. I made some coffee." Lyle's voice echoed down the long hallway.

Janine touched her throat with her left hand. She swallowed once, then again. Looked down at her right hand.

"Janine? You there?" Lyle's voice, closer now, had an edge of concern.

Janine cleared her throat, softly, then louder. She walked away from the closet, toward the hallway, to meet Lyle.

THE QUEEN IS DEAD
LONG LIVE THE QUEEN

THERE IS NO WAY I WANT to go to a party. Not now, not after hanging on, making it through the last few days the way I promised myself I would.

"I'm bushed, Clare," I say, yelling over the music from the band at the final supper and dance. "I've spent the last forty-eight hours smiling and talking. I've had it. I just want to go to bed. We're getting an early start tomorrow morning, remember? I want to be home by Monday afternoon."

"C'mon, Ingrid. Come with me. Most of this stuff was a big scam, anyway. Pretending we all look so great, lying about everything, fabulous careers, goddamn meaningful relationships. Even the old bags, the teachers who are still around, acting like they remember us. And worst of all, these little eighties girls, these snobby hostesses," she says, having just a tiny bit of trouble with the word hostesses, "who think they're so great because they've still got tight little asses and great boobs. Did you notice, Ingrid, did you notice that girls today have bigger boobs than when we were young?" Clare's mascara is making spidery black marks under her eyes, and little wisps of hair are stuck to her temples.

She drains her glass and leans toward me. "It's time to *really* party, girl. And the party I found for us isn't anything to do with the reunion. New places, new faces. Let's do what we do best. Forget all this small-talk shit and have some fun. You used to love parties. You couldn't say no to one."

I turn my head away from her.

"Don't say no, Ing. Come with me. If you don't, you'll have to get a cab to the hotel." Her eyes narrow, and a smile pulls up one corner of her lip. "I've got the keys, and I'll drive myself if you won't come."

I face her again. "Blackmail, Clare."

"No, no." Clare swings her head back and forth, back and forth, a shaggy blond pendulum. "It's all a question of debts, Sis." Her voice is slow and careful, and her eyelids lower each time the band hits a loud note. "'Member all the times I chauffeured *you* around, eh. Don't forget about *that*." A fine shower of saliva hits my cheek as she stresses the last word. "And I still cover for you, don't I? Don't I, eh, Ing?"

I pick up my purse. "Just for an hour, then. One hour, and then we go back to the hotel."

"Deal. One hour. Hey, wait a sec."

She turns around and fills her glass from the bottle of white wine on the table, then yanks one of the balloons from the centrepiece of red and gold carnations and red balloons. She slips the end of the curling ribbon under the belt of her dress. The balloon bobs along beside her head as we walk, CRESSWELL HIGH REUNION 1968–1988 written in gold letters on the puckering rubber.

In the parking lot, Clare hugs her purse against her chest with the same hand that holds her glass. She digs in the white leather bag with her free hand. Splashes of wine hit the front of her dress, drop inside her purse. The balloon dips and weaves with her movements.

She finally tosses me the keys, and when I unlock the
door, she gets in, her skirt hiked up around her thighs. She's
still looking through her purse.

"I've got the address in here somewhere."

I pull out of the parking space, stop at the exit of the lot,
and look over at my sister. "This is hard, Clare. And you're
not helping. You said you'd help if I came with you." I wait.
"So which way, Clare? Whose place is it, anyway?"

Clare hasn't lifted her head from the depths of her
purse. "Dunno. But it's gonna be good. Phil told me about
it."

"Phil?"

"Phil. Short guy, big schnozz. I was dancing with him
after supper. I think I remember him from the grade ahead
of me. You must know him; he says he worked on the
yearbook committee with you. Ah-ha!" She holds up half of
an envelope. "634 Arnold," she says, then rolls down the
window, letting the warm June air rush into the car. The
balloon is swept up, its ribbon tail pulled out of Clare's belt,
and it escapes through the window, into the night.

The party is hot, noisy, crowded, in a big old house in a row
of big old houses. As soon as we get inside Clare disappears,
elbowing her way through the crush of the hallway like she's
been here before, knows the place.

I edge my way from room to room. There seem to be a lot
of them, rooms. They're all filled with people, mostly
strangers. I say hi how're you doing hot isn't it to a guy who's
vaguely familiar.

The house looks like it's half-renovated—some
woodwork stripped and sanded, some still layered in coats of
thick chipped cream-coloured paint. I get to the kitchen. It's
completely modern—all in white, with a cappuccino maker,
food processor with a bread kneading attachment, a row of
steel German knives on a metallic strip on the wall over the
red enamelled sink.

I see the counter, the jungle of bottles, the pools of melting ice cubes. I just stand and look, studying the familiar glass shapes, forcing myself to linger over the tallest one, let my eyes stay on its cool slim beauty for an extra minute, then I take a deep breath and reach out for a big plastic bottle of cola, something dark and fizzy. I fill the glass and, carrying it, manoeuvre through the hallway again, upstairs, to the bathroom.

Whoever is working on the house hasn't got to this room yet; it's still in its original state. The pedestal sink and clawfoot tub are yellowed and scratched, and lots of tiny white octagonal floor tiles are missing. The toilet is high and narrow, the handle shaped like a long teardrop.

I stare at myself in the clouded mirror of the wooden medicine cabinet. I'm glad it's so dark downstairs, everywhere except the kitchen. I won't go to the kitchen again, partly because of the unforgiving light, partly because I've already done my time at the counter.

Then I brush my hair, put on more lipstick, and take a minute to run my fingers over the lining in the bottom of my purse, reassured by the shape of the tiny cylinder under the satiny material.

When I come down from the bathroom, I look for Clare. I don't see her anywhere, so I push my way back through to the living room. It's been twenty minutes, a third of the sentence served. I step over groups of people sitting on the floor, making my way to the only unoccupied place in the room, the radiator. I smile brightly at nobody and everybody in the living room from my perch under the curtainless front window, bringing the glass to my lips every few minutes, feeling the sticky sweetness of the cola.

There's a sudden burst of extra noise at the front door, people laughing, a new crowd coming in. As they file past, carrying cases of beer, I see him.

He stops at the living-room door and surveys the scene,

not smiling, just looking from face to face. I sit up straighter. At first glance I think he hasn't changed much, just filled out.

His hair is longer. No grey, just shiny black, straight, parted in the centre and hanging long and loose, emphasizing his high cheekbones and strong jaw line. Under the hall light I can see that there are shallow pits and ghosts of scars on his angular face. His eyes look around the room with a boldness I don't remember; calm, maybe even proud. He's as thin as he was twenty years ago, but with the thinness his body holds a kind of threat. Under his white T-shirt his shoulders are wide and square.

I realize my first impression is wrong; everything about him has changed.

His eyes pass over me, go on to the people lined up on the couch. He leaves the doorway. I sit there, feeling something stirring in my chest, something moving like it's been asleep for a long time.

I think about getting up, following him, but he probably went into the kitchen. So I wait, watching the living-room doorway for him to reappear.

When I finally look away, back into the room, it seems to have grown hotter, darker, the music louder.

I start to feel disconnected, like I've wandered into some kind of giant hive, some swarming place with no exit. I pick up my purse. Even it feels unfamiliar, has somehow become huge and heavy when I wasn't looking.

If I can just make it upstairs, to the bathroom, I'll let myself do a few lines, just a few, then I'll be able to handle the kitchen, look for him, talk to him.

I rub my hand over the clasp of my purse. I deserve it. I've passed the test. The reunion is officially over now.

As I stand up, a tiny flare twinkles in the doorway, and in that brief flash the face I was watching for is illuminated. The match goes out, and his face is hidden again, but each time he takes a drag on the cigarette I see the outline of his features, jerky, distorted, like a strobe light is passing over it.

31

I have to pass him to get to the stairs, to the bathroom. I make my way across the room. He's leaning against the door frame. He looks down at me as I hesitate in front of him, and a slow smile parts his lips.

I lift my eyebrows. "Hi," I say, loud enough to be heard over the heavy bass beat of the music. "Hi, Russell."

"Ingrid," he says.

I realize I've been holding my breath. "I didn't know if you'd remember me."

He keeps looking at me. I can't read the expression on his face.

"Well," I say, "it *has* been twenty years." My smile is pulling at my lips. They hurt. I put my hand up to brush my hair off my shoulder, and something crackles against the tips of my fingers. I look down. A white tag is still stuck on the front of my dress, over my left breast. Big red HELLO, smaller letters stating *My Name Is*, and then, underneath, INGRID, in the neat black letters I'd printed before the dinner.

My smile doesn't change, but it's hard work.

"Ingrid Finnbogason. I was in a few of your classes. Math. Mr. Schinkel; we called him Mr. Sphincter."

Russell nods. "The Snow Queen." His eyes are hooded; still no clue what's going on behind them.

I dismiss the title with a wave of my hand, the stirring in my chest bubbling up, strange joy at the knowledge that he does remember after all.

"God. I can't believe how much I wanted to win that. Was I shallow or what? I almost failed my spring exams because of all the time I spent campaigning in February. The Snow Queen." I snort.

There's a sudden drop in the noise level in the room when the music ends. I realize I've been shouting. My throat suddenly feels narrow, my tongue too big for my mouth. I can't think of anything to say, look away from Russell's eyes, over toward the shelving unit that holds the stereo, hoping someone will put something else on. Something to fill the cobweb of space between us.

The space stretches, pulls in. He's still looking at me. "I'll be right back," I say, and leave, toward the stairs. Half of me wants him to be gone when I come back, the other half desperately wants him to be there, waiting for me.

All I can think of is the last night I saw Russell. Those minutes are standing there, so clear at the front of my mind that I'm sure the imprint is pushing out on my forehead for him to see, to remind him of what I let happen.

Russell came to our school just after Thanksgiving. Even though he was in two of my grade twelve classes, I never talked to him. But then no one talked to him; even the teachers didn't call on him or ask him anything. Russell didn't talk either, didn't ask anyone about homework assignments, didn't smile or laugh when someone did something stupid in class. He was like a nocturnal creature, sitting mute and unmoving, camouflaged, blending in with the other guys in his jeans and plaid flannel shirt, unnoticed, but noticing everything.

There was something I saw, or actually that I couldn't quite see, that made me wonder about him, try to figure out why he was so silent, so unaffected by everything around him. There were times when I looked up from my desk, from whatever I was working on, and saw his profile, and I would get this strange feeling. Like he possessed a kind of atmosphere, an aura, like nothing could touch him, nothing could hurt him.

I pulled out his file one day when I was putting away some papers in the guidance counsellor's office. The girls in grade twelve General Business had this "opportunity" to work in the office one period each week, simple stuff like filing and answering the phone and typing announcements. Practising some of the skills we'd supposedly be using after graduation.

I pulled out the metal drawer marked H–L, and riffled through the files until I found him. LINKLATER, Russell Elias. Standing in the empty office, I opened the thin file and read through as fast as I could.

There was the school admittance form listing address, date and place of birth, all the usual. Russell had been born on the Long Point Reserve, and under parents/legal guardians there were a lot of crossed-out names and finally *Mrs. A. Linklater (Aunt)* had been pencilled in. There was a report from the Guy Hill Residential School in The Pas, where Russell had been for grades ten and eleven. Then there was a medical report, about a hip operation, and a statement from Mrs. Justine Hogg, with Child and Family Services, recommending that Russell not return to The Pas immediately, but remain in foster care in Winnipeg until the physiotherapy was completed. At the bottom of the typed sheet she had scribbled a short paragraph, something about high intelligence, artwork indicating sensitivity but shadowed by dark undercurrents, typical social work jargon.

I started to look at the test cards and drawings held together with a paper clip, but heard voices in the outer office and shoved the file back where it belonged.

The next day I watched Russell come into class, saw how he walked to his desk with a slight tilt and sway, saw how he looked out the window for most of the period, staring at the black, leafless branches of the oak outside the second-floor window, his eyes still, but rushing away at the same time. And there was something about him I wanted to know; I wasn't sure what it was, but I thought that maybe if I kept watching him, thinking about him, I might figure it out.

But I was also going steady with Terry Osachuk. After a few minutes I told myself to stop thinking about Russell Linklater. Instead I thought about what Terry and I had done on the old couch in his rec room last weekend, where we'd had our hands and mouths, with his parents right above us in the living room watching television. I thought about what we'd do the coming weekend, who would be having a party, if Terry and I would have enough money between us to get someone with an I.D. to buy us a mickey of rye, if our friend Milo would be able to score a dime bag, and if he did, would he share it with us. I drew hearts with *T* and *I* intertwined up and down the margins of my math book, trying not to glance over at Russell.

It was the Easter long weekend, and the weather turned mild. Word about a party started circulating, a big open house over at Chris Chester's. He lived in one of the mansions down by the river, and his parents were in Europe for two weeks.

Terry and I rolled in about 10:30, when the party was just getting under way. We'd been drinking vodka and Seven, and on the way over I'd rolled a few joints, some really strong grass cut with opium that had blown us away the night before.

After about an hour I started feeling sick, needed some fresh air. I told Terry I was going outside for a minute. He was sitting cross-legged on the floor of a room lined with bookshelves, the library I guess, holding in a lungful of smoke. He squinted up at me, and passed me the joint. I took it and found a set of French doors covered with sheer curtains, opened the doors and stepped out onto a huge flagstone patio. It was surrounded by a waist-high brick wall.

I shut the door on the light and music and loud voices and walked straight ahead, to the end of the patio, and stood in the coolness, taking deep breaths and trying to hold down the queasiness in my stomach. I heard something, maybe the scrape of a shoe, maybe the feathery touch of a hand in hair, and turned towards it.

Russell was sitting on the wall at the far edge of the patio, his legs hanging over, looking out at the blackness that must have been the river.

"Hey, Russell," I said. I'd never seen him at any parties, any dances at the school or community-club canteen.

He nodded.

"Whatcha doin' out here, Russell? Party's inside." It was easy to talk in the dimness, with the vodka and grass at work.

"I like it better out here," he said.

"But there's no party." I walked to him, holding out the joint. "C'mon, let's start one."

Russell turned and slid off the wall, sort of pulling one of his legs over like it wouldn't do what he wanted it to. He looked at my hand, but didn't reach out.

I put my arm down, studied his face in the faint light from inside the curtained French doors. "So. What do you plan to do? After graduation, I mean. Only a few more months. Are you going home? Up north?"

Russell gave me this sideways jabbing look. Sort of suspicious, or maybe just surprised.

"I don't know for sure," he said. Then he looked into my face, without lowering his eyes or looking away like he did in school. There was something else about him that night, but I told myself I was just seeing him differently, in the soft blackness of night, instead of under the buzzing harshness of the fluorescent lights in school. And I definitely had on a buzz of my own.

"Maybe I'll go back. But there's not much to do there."

I looked down at the twisted, glowing end of the joint, looked back up. "What will you do if you don't? Go back."

Russell took a few steps closer. "The place I'm staying now, they can get me a job. Delivering furniture. Pretty good money."

He had a nice voice. Low, deep, the shifting melody of northern Manitoba.

"Do you miss it? Home."

Russell tilted his head back and looked at the sky. "I miss some things. The people. The quiet." He looked at me. "Yeah. I miss it."

I held out the joint again, and this time stepped right in front of him.

His eyes dropped to the joint, and he took it, his fingertips grazing mine. He put it between his second and third fingers, like he was holding a cigarette, and held it to his lips. Then he took a little puff, blew it out.

"Inhale," I said, "and hold it in. For as long as you can."

This time he pulled hard, and I heard the little stopping click in his throat. I waited for him to pass the roach back to me, but he didn't. He just kept staring at me, and as I watched, I saw the slow blink, that second of disorientation that registered he'd zinged a hit. I smiled. He smiled back, and I saw his teeth for the first time. They were even and white.

He took another toke, then a third, and finally gave me the joint. I pinched the end and put it in the pocket of my jeans.

Russell turned back to the river, and I followed his eyes. I don't know how long we stood like that, looking at the water we couldn't see. I slowly realized Russell was making a sound, low, in his throat, like a dog catching wind of a rabbit. When the sound rose higher, I looked over at him. He started picking up his feet, one at a time, and setting them down again. Softly, at first, then harder, until it was a kind of stomping. He brought his arms out behind him and bent forward slightly. His eyes were closed.

I watched him, then picked up the beat and started stamping, softly, along with him. He must have heard my feet hitting the flagstones, because he raised his head and stopped, his eyes opening, glittering and a little wild. I stopped, too, and then his face relaxed, and he started again, moving his feet, but gently, slowly, just back and forth in front of me. I copied him again, watching him watching me.

Very faintly, I heard the sound of the Moody Blues from inside. Knights in White Satin. Russell and I were moving back and forth to the rhythm. We moved closer, and then we were standing together, barely moving, our arms around each other and my head against his chest. His heart was loud, almost louder than the music. The song seemed to go on and on, and after awhile I knew it was over, but we kept swaying together. I felt really warm and quiet, and all of a sudden I knew that was what I'd been trying to figure out all those times in class, sneaking glances at Russell. I knew that he could give me something, something I needed, something that started off with this quiet feeling, something to make me feel that everything was really alright, that I didn't have to be scared about things anymore.

But before I lifted my head off his chest to look up at him, see what I wanted to see, light and music spilled over us, and we were caught in glare and crushing noise.

"Hey, lookit," someone yelled. "Hey Ter, you better get over here, man. Your old lady's out here with the Indian."

I don't remember if Russell and I stepped away from each other or not, just that Terry was suddenly standing there, in the doorway, and he was yelling. "What's going on? Get your fucking hands off her, you asshole. Leave her alone."

I knew exactly what was going to happen, I knew Terry, but I was caught in the blaze of his face, the working of his jaw. It seemed to take him ten minutes to cross the few steps of the patio, but I did nothing to stop him. I stood there, waiting, hearing the echoes of his words collecting high above me, up in the bare tops of the trees that hung over us.

There must have been enough distance between Russell and me for Terry to get in, and raise his elbow, and his fist, and then Russell dropped down, out of my line of vision, like someone had cut his legs off. The patio seemed to fill with people, and I was pushed backwards, against the stone wall, and I heard soft thuds and gasps that stopped and started, stopped and started, and I knew what was happening to Russell.

Then I was vomiting over the wall, into prickly bushes, spattering the new desert boots I'd sneaked out of Clare's closet, and I remember hearing someone say, maybe it was

Terry, maybe not, next time you'll remember to stick to squaws.

Russell never came back to school after that.

I look at myself, again, in the mirror over the sink. I've got the vial out, but I'm just holding it. I think I've been standing here a long time.

Someone bangs on the door. Hurry up, willya. Whaddya doing in there, laying an effin' egg?

I take my mirror out of my make-up bag and put it on the closed toilet seat. I lay out two lines and roll up a five tightly and get down on my knees and do the lines, quick and neat, then I lick off the mirror and put it and the bill and the vial back in my purse. I stand up and glance at my face again, take out my lipstick and slide it over my lips. It goes on smooth, slick. I keep coating it on until there's a loud thud against the door and this time a moan Jesus H Christ come on.

When I open the bathroom door a skinny redhead who looks like a babysitter I used when the boys were little pushes past me and prances in on the pointy toes of her scuffed white cowboy boots, unzipping her jeans before I even close the door.

Russell isn't where I left him. I don't see him anywhere until I go into the kitchen. It doesn't bother me anymore, the kitchen.

He's leaning against the counter beside the sink.

"I'm back," I say.

He studies my face, then reaches up and touches the edge of my right nostril with his knuckle. "Still a snow queen, eh, Ingrid?"

I just stand there, smiling. My lips feel good, natural this time.

He smiles back. It's a great smile. That smile could mean a lot of things. It gives me one push, low, in my abdomen. A sweet throb I've been missing.

I haven't felt it since I quit drinking. No desires, no fantasies, no sex for over a year. At first, I thought it was because I felt so sick, so dried out, everywhere. I knew it would hurt, couldn't think about it. But even when I started to feel better, still nothing.

Now I'm standing here, looking up at Russell's face, wanting to touch his flawed skin, take his hands and put them on my own cheeks and hold them there, let him feel the heat all over my body, let him make me feel like I'm O.K.

My mouth is dry. I look at the counter beside Russell, then step around him and get myself a cup of coffee from the urn. I take a sip; it's hot and strong. My lipstick leaves a pleated imprint on the outside of the thick white mug.

"Tastes good," I say.

Russell takes the cup from my hand, looks at the lipstick stain on the rim. Slowly, he puts his mouth over the lipstick, settles his own lips over the red and takes a long drink, his eyes never leaving mine.

"You're right," he says, then he hands the cup back to me and glides out of the kitchen.

And I'm left looking down at the cup, wanting him to come back to me, to put his lips on mine, brushing them, the way he so gently touched these brilliant, phantom others.

HOLES

"WHAT COULD YOU SEE?" she keeps asking me. "Could you see her tongue? Her teeth? That yucky little thing that hangs down? What could you see, Mom? Tell me!"

She's lying beside me on the bed, holding the Black Magic Chocolates box of pictures, a legacy from my grandmother. It's late, but neither of us can sleep.

The black-and-white picture that mesmerizes her is small and creased. A young woman stands outside a wooden building. It could be a hen house or a tool shed or her home. She wears a stained apron over a long wrinkled dress; a kerchief covers her hair, and she has turned away from the camera, her hand over part of her face. The nails look dirty, broken, but it's still clear that the fingers are delicate.

There is a name, Roia, and one sentence on the back of the picture. No date, no indication of place. Roia. The strange name Baba rolled off her tongue; she smiled when I tried but couldn't say it like her.

And the words, the Ukrainian words that my baba read to me once, when I was about the same age as my daughter is now. A year or two before Baba started shrinking, withering, finally becoming a silent part of her bed, with a tiny face hard to make out, hidden among the faded pink and yellow roses on the pillowcase.

"Look, look at her hand, Kathleen," she'd said. Like me, she had trouble with names, calling me Cat-a-leen. I leaned closer, studying the picture.

"What's she doing, Baba?" I had asked.

Baba turned the picture over, read the words. "She is covering the hole in her chick," she read. She said it clearly, calmly.

I remember saying "chick, chick? What chick?" Until Baba slapped the side of her own lined face, hard. "Chick, Cataleen, chick. She had a hole."

I don't know if I asked anything about the hole. How could I not have? Wouldn't I have had the same questions as my daughter?

Last week my daughter asked me about the words on the back of the picture. She's six, caught up in letters and sounds and the magic of words. I told her about my baba's language, what Baba had told me the words said.

I wish I hadn't; she won't let it drop. Three times today I've seen her looking at herself in the cracked mirror over the dresser beside my bed, stroking her own round cheeks.

Now, lying stiffly on the hot rumpled sheets, she keeps asking about the hole. And she has another question. Her voice is soft. "Did she have a lump, Mom?" she asks, still looking down at the picture in my hand, her straight shiny hair hiding her face. She asks the question like she asks if it's going to rain, if we can have pancakes for breakfast. But there's something else, a tiny intake of breath afterwards.

"Did she? Did she have a lump in her cheek, Mom? And then the doctor cut it out?"

We are both very still. The room is hot. Flies throw themselves against the screened black. I reach behind me to push the curtain aside, let some air in.

"I don't know, baby," I say. I try to hug her, but she

pulls away. My hands hang in the air between us. "Let's put the pictures away, turn out the light."

"Can I phone Daddy?"

"No. It's too late, he'll be sleeping. But he'll be here tomorrow, don't worry. And after you guys drop me off he'll take you back to his place. Just like we arranged."

"Do you think everyone could see down her throat? Can you see inside, when they take the lump out?"

I pry the picture out of her fingers and toss it back in the box. Damn.

"No, honey, you can't see inside. They fix the skin again. I told you that. You can hardly tell."

"But they didn't fix hers."

"No. But that was a long time ago. And maybe it wasn't the same thing. Maybe it was something else."

This time when I put my arms out she comes into them. I hold her and finally she softens against me, pushing the box of pictures away with her foot, pushing and kicking at it until it falls off the bed with a thud.

Later, something wakes me. In the darkness she is sitting up, looking down at me. I can see her eyes, the way they look at the part of my breast above my nightgown, the skin smooth and unblemished for this final night.

I know that she's wondering about tomorrow. If when they let her in to my room, she will be able to see my heart.

THE CARD

THE CARD ARRIVED ON MONDAY. The envelope was cream coloured, heavy, Queen Elizabeth's impassive purple profile on the stamps. Inside the circle of the postmark Sandra read LONDON S.W.I. 14 XII'72

Had the card shown up on one of the other four weekdays, Sandra would have glanced at the name, then shoved it in the desk drawer with the rest of the mail to be forwarded to the Ellices, the owners of the house, in Seattle for a sabbatical year.

But the envelope had arrived on a Monday. Mondays were always hard; she needed a distraction on Mondays. This Monday was particularly bad, the first Monday in the worst month, January. So Sandra steamed open the thick envelope.

She held it by one corner, slowly moving it back and forth over the kettle until the edges of the sealed flap had started to peel up just the tiniest bit, then more and more.

Sandra unplugged the kettle, sat down at the gleaming oak dining table, and carefully pried the flap up, sliding the card out of its snug, foil-lined home.

45

It was a Christmas card, subdued, in very good taste. No overly jolly Santas or mischievous kittens wrapped in red and green ribbon, no cherubic children looking skyward through a frosted window. The card matched the envelope; simple heavy cream. A delicate sketch of a dove holding a small branch with one perfect green leaf. Sandra opened the card. A photo fell out.

It was a man and a little girl. They sat under a tree, on a wooden bench. The child was on the man's lap, her head against his chest. She looked down at her skirt, at her hands folded neatly together. There was almost a smile on her lips, as if she were shy, or perhaps coy, refusing to look at the camera. The man was slight, trim, with wide eyes and thick blond hair, falling loosely over his forehead. His arms encircled the child easily, naturally. Sandra's mouth began to tremble. She pressed her fingers against it, then put the picture down, and looked back to the card.

Inside, in gold, the word PEACE. Under the word the names Richard and Deborah in black ink.

On the opposite side was a brief correspondence, written in the same spidery letters as the names, with what Sandra deduced would be a thin-nibbed, tortoiseshell fountain pen.

"We had a quiet summer," the careful writing said, "and the first term went more smoothly than I dared hope. Deborah is coping as well as can be expected; it will take us both some time. You must make another trip to England soon—or Deborah will be all grown up! Thank you for your kind words of condolence. R."

Sandra read it through another time, letting her eyes rest on each word. Then she gently slid the card back into the envelope and licked the still-sticky glue of the flap. A small part of her mind told her that her tongue was licking the same surface as someone named Richard.

The thought comforted her, briefly, the tiny connection

of her tongue with another tongue, one that belonged to someone in a place far from Manitoba's unforgiving and endless winter, with a life so different from her own, and yet similar. The coping.

She pressed the flap closed with the heel of her hand, and then she put her head down on the cool dark wood and wept.

She tried not to blame Harley. She told herself it wasn't his fault that she was stuck in an elegant but drafty rented house in a treeless cul-de-sac at the end of a new housing development, close to the computer training centre where he had been transferred that fall. Wasn't his fault that the wind howled up and down the barren street, hour after hour, day after day. It isn't Harley's fault, she said to herself, over and over, for those first few months in the house. It's nobody's fault. Things just happen.

Some days nothing moved on the curved street at all. Sandra knew, because she sat in front of the picture window, on the soft beige loveseat, and watched, from the time Harley left for work until she started supper.

"Any mail?" Harley asked. He hadn't lifted his head, eating the shepherd's pie with a sense of urgency, as if someone might snatch his plate away if he didn't finish quickly.

"Just a Christmas card."

"A Christmas card? A little late, isn't it?"

"It's late because it came from England."

Harley stopped chewing, looked up. "Who do we know that lives in England?" He glanced at her clean plate. "Not eating?"

"Nobody. We don't know anybody that lives in England. We don't even know anybody that lives on this bloody street."

"Now, Sandra," Harley said, picking up his fork and

pointing it at her. "Don't start. You know I have to go where they send me. You know that. I don't have a lot of say, I—"

"You do so, Harley. You're the top computer programmer for your damn company. You can't pretend that you don't have any rights, any choice. We never stay anywhere. I never have a chance to meet anyone, make real friends." She dug the serving spoon into the shepherd's pie and lifted it into the air, balancing a large wet chunk of ground beef and carrots, topped with mashed potatoes.

"Sandra," Harley warned. "Don't you—"

He ducked as the food flew past his head, then turned to watch it slide down the wallpaper behind him, leaving a dark greasy trail over the twisting vines of ivy. He stood up, throwing his fork onto his plate. It bounced off and hit the floor with a dull ping.

"That's enough, Sandra. Enough. The Ellices rented—"

"Enough? Hah! I'll show you enough." She picked up the Corning Ware casserole. As she started to raise it above her head, Harley moved towards her with unusual speed, and grabbed hold of the bowl, his larger hands over hers.

"Put. It. Down. Sandra." His voice came from between his teeth.

They stood there for perhaps ten seconds, staring into each other's eyes. Then Sandra looked down to Harley's mouth, seeing a fleck of mashed potato on the right side of his bottom lip. For one wild second she imagined leaning forward and putting out her tongue and licking it off, wondered what Harley would do.

But she didn't want the creamy smoothness of the potatoes in her mouth. She wanted to remember the taste of the envelope for as long as she could. She relaxed her grip on the bowl, let Harley take it out of her hands and set it back on the table.

When Harley sat down on the edge of the bed that night, Sandra turned over, facing the wall.

"Look, Sandra," he said, his back to hers. "You know you always get hurt when you try to make friends. People always let you down. It's human nature. It's easier to not get involved in the first place. Remember Beverly Carter? Remember that mess with the Reimers? You're always getting yourself into trouble."

Sandra felt him tugging at the spread. "You're your own worst enemy, Sandra. You're a poor judge of character. Where would you be, if I wasn't around to bail you out?"

After a minute's silence, Sandra answered, her voice low. "I'm starting to think about it."

"What's that supposed to mean?"

"It means, I'm starting to think about my life without you, Harley. I imagine myself finally getting my teaching degree, getting a job, making friends for myself, without you stopping me from doing anything that makes me happy." She took a wavering breath. "Without you taking everything away from me."

Harley didn't move for another minute. Then he slid under the covers, still keeping his back to Sandra. As he pulled his knees up, his bottom touched Sandra's. She instantly pulled away, to the very edge of the mattress.

She lay there, listening, watching the glowing hands of the clock on the bedside table. Waiting. The mattress pitched as Harley tossed himself onto his back, and almost immediately the low snuffling sounds started.

She slowly turned over, and studied his large head in the shadowy light from the pale square of the window. Then she reached out and, with her thumb and forefinger, grasped one long greying hair on his high forehead. She waited until the next jagged snore crescendoed, then gave the hair a hard yank. It came away easily.

Harley jerked, mumbled, and rolled over to his right side again.

In the silence, Sandra licked her lips, over and over, remembering the gumminess of the glue, feeling the slide of her tongue. Richard, she thought.

The next morning Sandra got the envelope out again. She looked at the return address in the upper left-hand corner, ran her fingers over the words. R. Albon, No. 22 Chillington Close, London, England.

Sandra tried to imagine a house on a street called Chillington Close. She thought of a friendly red brick, a wooden door with a brass knocker—a lion's head or maybe a lady's fine-knuckled hand—open windows showing a whisper of sheer white curtains, a flash of chintz on the furniture. The small, informal front garden was filled with wild masses of white daisies and pink phlox. The path to the front stoop had green mossy patches spreading over some of the stones, worn smooth by the footsteps of Richard and his daughter. Richard would wear well-polished Italian loafers, Deborah black patent shoes with a strap over the top.

Sandra raised her eyes to the empty whiteness outside her own window. Then she went to the kitchen drawer and took out a lined writing pad and a ballpoint pen.

"Dear Richard," she wrote. "You don't know me, but I feel that we have a lot in common."

She ripped the sheet off the pad, crumpled it and threw it onto the floor.

"Dear Mr. Albon," she started again. "Through mutual friends, the Ellices, (you may not be aware they are away for the year, in Seattle, Washington) I have heard of your . . ." She stopped, sucked the end of the pen, ". . . situation.

"I'm writing to wish you strength, and hope for the future. I've also experienced the loss of a loved one recently, and I know how despairing this time is. But with each month, I see a slight change. I don't think the hurt ever leaves entirely, but it does grow less barbed. I'm waiting, as I know you are, for the barbs to lie still, to lose their edge, so that they no longer prod and push.

"My thoughts are with you."

She read it over, considered throwing it out, wondering

if Richard Albon would think she was someone crazed, then quickly signed it, Sandra Murray, put it in an envelope, and sealed it. She addressed it and put on all the stamps she found in the drawer. She put her return address on the back of the envelope, wrote AIR MAIL along one side of the front.

Finally she put on her winter coat and boots and walked the two blocks to the mailbox. She put the letter in through the slot, then walked home, swinging her arms briskly.

February 10
Dear Mrs. Murray,

It was so good of you to write. It seems impossible to describe suffering a tragic loss to anyone who has not experienced it. Your few words were immensely appreciated. I do hope you are adjusting—may I be so bold as to inquire about the cause of your husband's death?

With Sincerity,
Richard Albon

February 20
Dear Richard, (I hope you don't mind)

It was kind of you to reply; I was worried that you would find my letter upsetting.

It was not my husband that died, but my child, a little girl about the age of yours. It was a tragic accident, and losing her so unexpectedly left me empty. I'm just now beginning to see my way out of the darkness.

I'm hoping to enrol in a spring session at the University of Manitoba; I need several more credits to complete my teaching degree. I think this commitment will help.

Say hello to your daughter for me; tell her
Manitoba is far behind England in watching for
spring!

Sincerely,
Sandra Murray
P.S. My husband and I are estranged.

March 15
Dear Sandra,

Spring is in full bloom here; Deborah and I
took a ride out to the countryside on the weekend.
It was lovely; she is a child who appreciates nature
and even at her young age is good company.

I admire your strength in resuming your studies. This time must be doubly difficult for you
without the support of your husband.

I was forced to return to my job (as you must
know from the Ellices, I am headmaster at St.
Belham's) immediately after the funeral, and I am
sure that it was my salvation.

While Peter was teaching at St. Belham's, I
learned a great deal about Manitoba. It is hard to
imagine such a climate, and I am quite enchanted
with the history of your province—those brave
pioneers, and the romanticism of settling a new
land!

I am trying to remember if Peter and Barb
mentioned you.

Deborah says to tell you that her favourite
spring flower is the daffodil. She would like to
know if you have daffodils in Canada.

—Richard

April 17
Dear Richard,

Tell Deborah that yes, we do have daffodils. The first green shoots should be up in a few weeks. They are hardy flowers, some even brave enough to poke up through the last traces of snow.

I was sorry to cancel my plans for spring session at the university. Unfortunately my husband did not approve, and since he controls the purse-strings, at least until I get on my feet, I will have to wait. I am hoping to get a part-time job, and that would give me the funds to take at least one summer course.

Please forgive my complaining.

I mentioned that my daughter died accidentally. How did you lose your wife?

I look forward to hearing from you.

—Sandra
P.S. Is Deborah a fan
of Winnie The Pooh?

May 2
Dear Sandra,

I was so sorry to read that you weren't able to take the course(s) you wanted. Hopefully it will work out for the summer.

I am in the thick of all our end-of-year activities. A busy time, but rewarding—seeing the older students graduate is always a pleasure.

Deborah is currently attending an infant day school. Next year she will begin her formal education; she imagines herself to be quite a young lady and often scolds me for my lack of expression in her bedtime stories. I must try harder! I am most fortunate to have a housekeeper who is wonderful with Deborah. Also my sister, who lives south, in

Maidstone, visits as often as possible, and Deborah is quite close to her.

My wife had a lingering illness; she was not herself for a number of years.

I am trying to picture Winnipeg in spring! Give me some details.

—Richard
P.S. Yes, Deborah loves
Winnie The Pooh and his entourage,
and we have shared an occasional
teatime of bread and "hunney."

May 30
Dear Richard,

I hope you will accept this little package for Deborah. They were my daughter's, and it gives me pleasure to pass them on to another little girl.

I started a part-time job at the beginning of the month. It is very simple, just a few hours every afternoon at a nearby bookstore, unpacking and shelving. Not overly exciting, but I have always loved reading, and feel a quiet pleasure in just being around books. Does that sound silly?

I've already arranged for my summer course —it feels wonderful to have some independence.

I know I sounded very negative about my husband in my last letter. After I sent it I felt I should have explained further.

For awhile I held him responsible for our daughter's death—he was driving. I think I've risen above that now, but things had been bad between us for long before the accident, and this past year I decided it was time I thought seriously about my future.

As to your question about spring in Winnipeg, it is very short, often wet, but wonderful after so many months of cold and snow. This spring is particularly important to me; it marks one year of grieving, and the time to begin again.

I planted flowers, geraniums and marigolds, along the back fence this weekend. They are plain plants, not at all glamorous, but . . . stalwart, somehow. I respect their vigour. And it is cheering to look out on some colour from my kitchen window. Until next time,

Sandra

June 19
My dear Sandra,

How thoughtful of you to send the delightful Pooh books. Deborah was thrilled with the collection. I have told her about our friend in Canada. The little drawing she has made is a thank you.

It means a great deal to me that you would part with such a special treasure.

I am so pleased about your job, and your pushing on with your plans at the university. Good for you. I thought of you when you mentioned your stalwart plants (and on reading back through your letters see that once before you spoke this way—the "bravery" of the daffodils). I realized that in much the same way I respect your determination to get on with life. But certainly I do not think of you as "plain," as you describe your garden. I have quite a clear image of you in my mind. Would you find it terribly forward if I asked you to send me a picture?

Only one week of school left, and then I will have the summer to spend with Deborah. In the past I often took on summer tutorials, but of course wouldn't think of it now.

Please write soon.

Richard

June 29

Dear Richard,

I received your letter today, and sat right down to write back. Is this soon enough?

No, I don't think it forward of you to ask for a picture. I'm sending one from a few years ago; I haven't felt inclined to take any pictures, or have any taken, this last year. My hair is longer now, and I'm a little thinner.

I was flattered that you thought of me as determined. I really think I'm heading in that direction, becoming stronger, making decisions on my own. For the first time in a long while I feel I have some control over my life.

I'll be starting my summer course next week, and looking forward to it. Great that you're planning to have the summer with Deborah. It's obvious that you're a loving and sensitive father.

Fondly,
Sandra

July 15

My dear Sandra,

I wanted to sit down and write you the moment I received your letter, but had to wait until today—I'll explain later.

First of all, I must tell you how I appreciated receiving your picture. Thank you. You are far lovelier than I had envisioned, but somehow . . . familiar. Maybe because I feel I'm starting to know you so well from your letters.

I waited to write to you until my plans were finalized. Back in May I was asked to speak at two conferences in Canada this summer, just before fall term commences. I didn't mention it as I really wasn't certain about many things.

I have just today found out that I will be in Toronto for three days, then fly to Regina for another two days. I have a day between the two symposiums, and I wondered if I could stop in Winnipeg and see you?

Is there any hope? The date would be August 20. Please write as soon as you can so that I can arrange my flights.

Yours,
Richard

P.S. My sister will be taking Deborah
to the seaside while I am gone.

July 26
Dear Richard,

Yes! August 20 would be wonderful. I'll have finished my course on the sixteenth, and my job at the bookstore is very flexible, so I'll be free as a bird. Do you have the whole day? A few hours? As soon as I know I'll make some plans. I think you'd really enjoy a visit to Lower Fort Garry, where the Red River Settlers first built a fort when they arrived in Manitoba. There are a number of other places I can think of to take you—I just realized I don't even know what you like to eat (apart from bread and hunney) so let me know and I'll make reservations for lunch.

I'll give you my phone number at the bookstore, in case there are any problems. I still go in most afternoons—luckily my class is in the mornings. It's easier to reach me there, as my boss will take any messages. The number is 204-555-3189.

It's hard to believe we'll be face to face in less than a month.

As always,
Sandra

August 6

Dearest Sandra,

I hadn't realized how I was holding my breath until I got your letter, saying you would be able to see me. I have arranged to arrive at the Winnipeg airport at 10:20 A.M. on August 20, and my flight leaves for Regina at 5:00.

In some ways I feel we are old friends, and in other ways complete strangers. I think this is all part of the delicious mystery.

I eat anything, and Lower Fort Garry sounds intriguing, but please don't make any lengthy plans. It will be a pleasure just to be with you.

You won't be able to write me again before I leave in ten days, but I have your number at the shop should there be any changes, although everything is tightly organized.

Until the 20th,

Richard

The mosquitoes had been gone for over a week; Sandra had started to sit out in the backyard after supper.

"I don't feel like doing the dishes tonight," she said, on the night of the nineteenth. She took a book and sat on a lawn chair on the small patio of cement blocks off the back door.

Harley had a nap on the couch, then got the newspaper and a beer and wandered out into the backyard. He sat in another lawn chair, across from Sandra, sipping his beer, looking at her over the top of the newspaper. He watched for a while before he noticed she wasn't turning the pages, just staring at the open book.

She looked up once, her eyes meeting his, but she immediately lowered her head over the book again.

About nine she stood up. "I'm going to bed."

"So early?"

She raised one corner of her mouth. "I'm tired. And I think I'll go out tomorrow, go downtown, do some shopping."

Harley took a drink, looking up at her.

Sandra put her book under her arm and went into the house.

Harley sat in the lawn chair until it was dark, just before ten. As he walked through the kitchen he set his empty beer bottle and the newspaper on the kitchen table, among the dirty dishes. He picked a chicken leg off the platter in the middle of the table, took a bite.

The phone on the wall beside the fridge rang. He looked at it, frowning, then threw the chicken back onto the plate and wiped his mouth with the back of his hand.

"Hello."

After a second, he said it again, louder. "Hello."

The man's voice on the other end was quiet. "Yes. Sorry. I'm afraid I've rung the wrong number. I was calling 555-8560."

"You've got it. Who did you want?"

"Oh." A slight hesitancy. "Actually, I was looking for Sandra Murray."

Harley looked at the receiver.

"Is this Sandra's home?"

"Yes. Who's this?"

"This is Richard. Richard Albon." The man's accented words were measured, cautious. "Could I speak to Sandra, please?"

There were a few seconds of silence, then Harley said, "Sandra's in the shower. I'll take a message."

"Perhaps I should tell her myself."

"I said I'll take the message." He waited, staring at the coiled wire of the phone.

"Right." The voice became determined, more forceful than before. "I had an appointment to meet Sandra tomorrow. I'm calling from Toronto. I've just been told there's been a change in my schedule. It's been set back a day. I tried to call her at the bookstore, but they were closed. I got this number from Information. I need to speak to Sandra about, about changing our . . . ah, our meeting, until the next day."

Harley reached for a kitchen chair, pulled it closer to the phone and sat down heavily.

"Richard who?"

He heard an intake of breath.

"I think it would be best to speak to Sandra personally. Hello? Could you have her call me?"

"Give me the number." Harley took a pen out of his shirt pocket and wrote the number on the edge of the newspaper. Then he hung up.

He went outside and looked at the sky. He found the Big Dipper, the Little Dipper, and Orion. Then he went back inside and walked down the hall, past the master bedroom, to a smaller room with white furniture trimmed in gold. Sandra was in the single bed, asleep on her back, one hand curled loosely up beside her cheek.

Harley closed the bedroom door. He went to the kitchen and dialled the number on the newspaper.

The phone was lifted before the first ring ended. Harley didn't wait for a hello.

"This is Harley Murray. Sandra's husband."

"Yes. I thought as much. Look, Sandra said, well, from the way she wrote I assumed you weren't together any more."

"You've been writing a long time?"

"Since January."

Harley nodded. "January," he said under his breath.

"I beg your pardon?"

"I was just thinking. Look, Sandra's still in the bathroom. I don't want her to hear me." He lowered his head, putting his forehead into his hand, leaning against the fridge. He kept his eyes closed while he talked. "I thought she was getting better."

"Better? She's been sick?"

"I guess you could call it that," Harley said slowly.
"Just recently? She didn't mention any . . ."
"No. She's been, well, sick, for a long time. Not
physically. Not physically sick," he repeated.

In the total silence, Harley heard the humming of the
fridge, felt its vibration along his arm.

"But, but surely, it was the shock. Of your . . . of losing
the child. Mr. Murray, are you still there?"

"She told you about a child? And about a car accident?"

"Well, yes. That was how we started writing, you see.
Because I'd lost my wife. And she spoke as if, as if she were
quite alone."

Harley made a choking sound, a cough. "I didn't know
it had started again."

"I'm sorry, Mr. Murray, I'm quite lost . . . I don't . . ."

"Look, Richard. Is it Richard? There was never a child.
Never an accident. Sandra has . . . delusions, they call them.
She's like a sponge. Soaks up other people's troubles; they
become hers. She can't tell the difference between what
really happens and what happens in her head."

He listened to the breathing on the other end of the phone.

"Look, you better not call again, O.K.? Or write. It will
only upset her. These things usually have a life span of
around six months. Then she forgets about them and goes
on to something else. She might try to write you again. I
can't keep an eye on all her movements. But it's better to
just ignore the letters."

"But her job, her studies . . ."

"All dreams. Just what she wishes she could do,
imagines herself doing." Harley cleared his throat, once,
twice, a third time. "You might as well know. I've been
advised, by her doctors, that it might be best to have her,
you know, professionally looked after. But I can't bring
myself to do it. I can't let her go."

"I'm awfully sorry." Richard's voice was low with shock.
"I had no way of knowing. Her letters were so . . . so lucid,
so intelligent. No sign of, of, well, anything amiss."

"She's a bright girl, my Sandra. I won't deny that. But look, I've got to go. I hear her getting out of the shower."

"Of course, but—"

Harley eased the receiver onto its hook. Then he went back to the smaller bedroom, opened the door and looked in. Sandra was still asleep, still in the same relaxed position.

Harley went into the room across the hall. This one was filled with shelves of books, a big upholstered chair, and a heavy wooden desk. He switched on the lamp on the desk, opened the top drawer. There was an assortment of pens, a few blank birthday cards, a chequebook, airmail paper and envelopes, a large roll of stamps.

The middle drawer had only looseleaf paper. But in the bottom drawer, under a binder and a text called *Learning Centres, A Guide for Effective Use in the Elementary Grades*, he found the letters, stacked in a neat blue pile. He picked them up, but didn't read them, just put them back where they had been, closed the drawer and stood looking down at the desk. He lifted up a framed picture. Sandra was grinning, touching noses with a little girl who had her arms wrapped around Sandra's neck.

The frame was a cheap wooden one, and gold-sprayed macaroni was glued haphazardly onto it. He turned the frame over. On the cardboard back, in round, perfect letters, was printed HAPPY MOTHER'S DAY TO MOMMY, LOVE SAMANTHA. In smaller letters, underneath, the teacher had printed Tiny Tots Nursery, May, 1972.

Harley looked back to the picture, running his thumb over and over Sandra's face. Then he set the picture back in its place and turned out the light, shutting the door behind him with a quiet but firm click.

TURNING THE WORM

THROUGH THE WINDOW over the kitchen table, Marianne can see the top of Shawna's head. The straight line of her scalp is gleaming white, and her shiny black hair hangs on either side of it like a thick, still curtain.

Marianne stops on the top step of the back porch, wanting Shawna to lift her head, wanting to see the curtains part, see the lit stage of her daughter's face.

But even when she puts her key in the lock, turns it with a noisy scrape, Shawna's head stays bent over her book. It's not until Marianne pushes the door closed with a swoosh of air and a dull slam that Shawna lifts her head. Her eyes, wide, startled, stare at Marianne. Then her eyelids drop the tiniest fraction, and she studies her mother's face.

"How come *you're* home so early?" she asks, raising her hands to her ears. Marianne sees that she has her headphones on, but with the headpiece around the back of her head, instead of over the top.

"It's not early. Almost six. Didn't you read my note? I

said I'd be back for supper." She glances at the table. "Homework on a Saturday?"

Shawna throws the earphones on the table beside her biology textbook, fiddles with the dials on her Walkman. "Early for *you.*" Shawna's latest habit is to emphasize key words. "And it's not *homework.* I have a test on Monday, *remember?*"

"Right. I brought you something from Wendy's," Marianne says, setting a white paper bag on the counter. "Tex-Mex chicken burger."

Shawna sighs. "I *told* you, Mother, I'm not *eating* that crap anymore. You know what's *in* there."

"Oh, yeah. I forgot." Marianne opens the fridge. "There's not much here. I'll shop after work on Monday. What do you want for supper?" She doesn't look at Shawna as she takes a bottle of cranberry juice out of the fridge.

"I'm not hungry." A vertical line appears between Shawna's clear grey eyes as she watches her mother carry the Wendy's bag and the juice to the table and sit down across from her. "I was *looking* for that sweatshirt."

Marianne opens the bag, pulls out a wrapped burger. "Sorry. You were asleep when I left." She pushes up the sleeves of the black Club Monaco sweatshirt and looks out the window over the table, shaking her head. "I should get started on the garden. It's almost too late to plant."

"I wasn't *asleep,*" Shawna says. "I *heard* you."

"Well, you were lying on your bed with your eyes closed."

"I was listening to *Kurt.*" Shawna raises her chin towards the Walkman in front of her.

"I wish you wouldn't," Marianne says. "Listen to that stuff."

A small smile pulls up the corner of Shawna's mouth. "I'm not *that* stupid, Mother," she says to the Walkman. "Even if *all* of Nirvana committed suicide, I wouldn't." Then she looks at Marianne, and her pupils shrink into sharp points. Marianne starts fiddling with the empty paper bag, folding it carefully, into smaller and smaller squares. Then she puts her hands in her lap, pulling at the sweatshirt sleeves, pulling them down so the cuffs cover even the backs of her hands.

"What were you *doing*, all afternoon at Lloyd's? And was *he* there? *Dunc?*"

Marianne unwraps the burger, looks at it, then wraps it up again. She unscrews the lid of the juice, takes a drink. "Yeah, he was there. And we were just sitting around, watching TV. Some Grand Prix thing. Lloyd's into car racing." She takes another drink, nudges the burger with her knuckle. "I'm not really hungry either. We ordered pizza around two. I had pizza. And a Pepsi."

Shawna stands up and heads to the stairs leading off the kitchen.

"I did, Shawna. I told you it was for sure this time." Her voice rises half an octave. "I gave you my word."

The girl starts up the steps. Marianne tilts her head towards Shawna's thin, straight back. "What, Shawna? What did you say?"

"NOTHING," Shawna yells, the word bouncing and ricocheting against the wood panelling in the dark stairway.

"I heard you say something," Marianne calls, but only the dying echo of "nothing" answers her.

Marianne is asleep when the phone rings. She opens her eyes and blinks into the darkness, then turns on the lamp on the bedside table as she picks up the phone.

"'Lo," she says, clearing her throat, glancing at the clock. "Hello?"

"Mare? Hey Mare, honey, where'd you go? Where're you at?"

Marianne struggles to a sitting position, picking up her Players Light from beside the phone. "I'm in bed, Dunc. It's after two." She taps the pack so the cigarettes and Safeway matches slide forward, and as she listens to the heavy, ragged breathing on the phone, she clamps the receiver between her ear and shoulder and lights a cigarette.

"So, Dunc?" she says, blowing out a long, thin ribbon of smoke. She watches it wreathe around the lampshade and disappear into the shadows beyond the bed. As she drops the cigarette package back onto the table, she sees a miniature paper tent, a folded piece of lined white paper beside the lamp. She wonders how she missed it when she got into bed. She unfolds it and looks at what's written on the torn scribbler page, then lays it on her stomach.

"I woke up, and I didn't know where you were, Mare. I was all alone." The thick voice threatens to choke itself.

Marianne puts the cigarette between her lips, sits up straighter. She reaches out one finger and touches the paper.

"I just went home, Dunc. Remember? That's all. I just went home. I had to check on Shawna." The cigarette rises and falls in the clipped waves of her words.

"Can I come over?"

"Go back to bed, Dunc. Sleep it off." She waits. She can hear the blood pounding in her ear, pressed against the phone. "And Dunc?" She inhales, holds it until her lungs start to ache, exhales. "Never mind."

"But I need you now, babe."

Marianne takes a coffee mug from beside the phone. She looks into it, then throws her cigarette into the scummy beige liquid. "No you don't. Now quit crying, and go to sleep." She slumps back against the pillow. "Everything'll be O.K." Her voice is softer, slower, now. "It'll all be O.K." It's the voice she used on Shawna, years ago. When Shawna still believed her when she said everything would be alright.

"It's O.K.," she murmurs, one last time, then gently places the receiver down, reaches beside the bed and unplugs the phone. She looks at the paper again, smoothing out the one crease line, then props it against the lamp, and lies down on her side, her eyes fixed on the brief message.

On the way downstairs the next morning, Marianne glances into Shawna's room. She can just see the top of Shawna's head, in the mess of clothes and books and quilts on the bed.

Standing in the kitchen, Marianne drinks a glass of orange juice, but the inside of her mouth still feels dry, as if she's been running for a long time. She passes her tongue over her lips and goes out to the backyard, picking up the garden fork that's been leaning against the side of the house since the beginning of May.

At the edge of the rectangular, weedy patch, Marianne puts the ball of her foot on the top of the fork, and pushes.

With a satisfying slide, the thick tines break through the hard topsoil. She turns the fork over, and breaks at the damp clumps of black dirt. She digs and turns again, and again, surprised at the richness of the soil under the surface. She feels a tight, almost pleasant pulling across her back.

When she turns over the fourth clump, she sees an earthworm burrowing frantically through the mud caught on the fork. She kneels and pulls off the fat, grey-pink worm, encased in wet dirt. She puts it into the cup of her hand, watching it work its way around the rough edges of her palm. She thinks about the day before, at Lloyd's, and about Dunc's voice, already loud and hoarse by the middle of the afternoon.

"Watch her. Hey, watch her, Lloyd. She'll eat the worm."

"Quit shittin' me, man."

"C'mon, Mare, eat the worm. Lloyd doesn't believe me."

Marianne had set her can of Diet Pepsi on the floor beside the couch and looked at the bottle of mescal in the middle of the coffee table. The thick ribbed slug in the bottom of the bottle was magnified by the golden liquid.

"No."

"Do it, Mare." Dunc walked over to Marianne, sat down on the couch beside her. "Eat it, baby. Show Lloyd."

Marianne kept staring at the worm. "Cut it out, Dunc. I said no." She picked up the can of Pepsi, took a sip. "I only did it once, anyway."

Dunc hooted. "Who're you kidding? You did it more than once." He held up his hand, fingers outstretched. "That New Year's Eve party out at the cabin." He folded down his thumb. "When we were out in the boat, fishing with Rick." His index finger went down. "The time in Bemidji, and, oh yeah," his third and fourth fingers bent over at the same time, "at your friend's place, what's-her-name, Mildred or whatever, from Safeway." He waved his little finger triumphantly.

"Millicent," she said.

"What?"

"Millicent. Her name was Millicent."

The little finger kept waving in front of her face. Dunc was grinning now. He picked up the bottle and rocked it from side to side. The worm floated upwards half an inch, then settled slowly and heavily to the bottom. "It's cawwwwling, you, Mare," Dunc said in a singsong voice.

Marianne got to her feet. "It's calling *you*, Dunc." She looked down at him, at the dark thinning hair on the top of his head. "Eat the bloody worm yourself," she said, picking up Shawna's sweatshirt and pulling it over her head. "I'd rather have a Wendy's Classic."

Marianne looks at the squirming earthworm in her palm, then brings her hand to her face, and sniffs at the strong, cool odour of freshly dug soil.

The only worm she's smelled before was from the bottom of the bottle. Thinking about that other worm, her mouth is filled with a salty iron taste, but it's all confused with other tastes, tears, and blood, and semen, on the back of her tongue, down her throat.

Without warning, she turns her head and spits onto the ground beside her, and wipes her mouth with her bare arm. As she leans back on her heels, she hears a small rustle from the pocket of her cutoffs. She thinks about the lined paper there, the two capital A's and seven-digit number, all in Shawna's clear, round style. She remembers helping Shawna learn to print letters and numbers, her own big hand, steady back then, over Shawna's little-girl, almost boneless fingers.

Marianne picks up the worm and turns it over. It finally lies still, and she breathes in the clean dark smell again, inhaling deeply, as if it can take away the taste in her mouth.

Then she gently tips her palm, down, toward the garden. She sits on her knees, one hand fingering the paper in her pocket, and watches until the last tip of the pointed tail, like a satiny pink tongue, disappears, slipping beneath the surface smooth and easy as a cool sip of water on a hot day.

FLOWERS FOR THE BRIDE

THE WOMEN IN MY FAMILY cried a lot.

They each had a different way of crying. Gram would hunch over and stare at the floor, whispering and shaking her head, letting the tears just run down her face.

My mom cried quietly too, but she never let the tears get going. Her eyes would get big and shiny, and her mouth would twist into a skinny line, and she'd start clattering dishes in the sink or pushing the sweeper back and forth, back and forth, even if the rug was already clean.

Auntie Brenda was the noisy one. She'd sob real loud, with big hiccupy noises coming from her throat. Her nose ran, and she'd need a tea towel if she was really feeling sorry about something.

Every night when I got into bed, between the soft flannel sheets my mom spread over the scratchy chesterfield in the living room, I tried to stay awake as long as I could, looking toward the bright rectangle of light, listening to the laughing and crying and talking in the kitchen. The voices went up and down, and ever since I was little I'd known that the time to pay attention was the down voices. I could fall asleep to the loud sounds, the interrupting and the arguments about silly things like the best way to bleach freckles or who was supposed to be on *The Ed Sullivan Show* that Sunday. But the best stories were the ones told in whispery voices. A lot of those stories were about passing out.

Auntie Brenda talked around a mouthful of toast. "I heard that Stella passed out in the middle of the doctor's office, when they told her it was the tumour, come back again. This time she'll have to get it all out, her you-know-what, and she thinks Frank won't stay with her, once it's gone."

"I tell you," my mom said, "I nearly passed out when I saw Irene with guess-who at the early show." Her voice was just a bit louder than the thump and slide of the iron. Every night she starched and ironed a white cotton blouse to wear under her usherette's uniform for her evening job at the Deluxe Theatre. During the day she worked at Woolworth's. "Bold as can be, hanging on to his arm and carrying on like she didn't care he had a wife sitting at home waiting for him."

Gram's words were echoed by the rattle of the peas she was shelling into a coffee tin in her lap. "Down I would go, right down, first thing I put my feet on the floor in the morning. Passed out every day for that whole year. Doctor says the change does that to some."

Passing out seemed pretty common among the women I heard about from the kitchen. Women passed out, came around, and went on with their lives.

My grandpa, Pop, had been sick forever. I had never seen him standing up; he was always lying in the double bed upstairs, in the bigger bedroom at the front of the house. Mom and Auntie Brenda shared the one at the back.

Pop was the only man in our house. I had a dad, once, but he left a long time ago, and I've only seen him in a picture. It was a wedding picture that my mom kept at the bottom of her sweater drawer; when no one was around I would take the picture out. It wasn't a wedding picture like some of the ones I'd seen at my friends' houses. There was no fancy frame, no covering of glass, just a grey cardboard folder. My mom wasn't wearing a long white dress, and she didn't have a veil. She had an ordinary green dress on, and she was holding a bunch of flowers in front of her. Lilacs. We had an old lilac bush in our backyard.

Once Auntie Brenda snuck in and saw me looking at the picture.

"Those flowers do a pretty good job, don't they?" she said, smiling at me in this mean way that meant any minute she was going to give my hair a yank or say something to make me feel bad, something about my teeth or how skinny I was.

"What do you mean?" I asked.

"You'll figger it out pretty soon," she said. Auntie Brenda was only eight years older than me, and my mom was eight years older than her. Sometimes when Auntie Brenda made me cry Mom told me that Auntie Brenda was just jealous, that she was the baby of the family until I came along, and she'd had her nose out of joint ever since. I didn't know how anyone could have their nose out of joint, but I guessed it must hurt, and that's why Auntie Brenda was always so miserable.

One morning just after Christmas Auntie Brenda woke me up. It was really early, still dark in the living room.

"Come on, get up, Suzette," she said, shaking my shoulder.

"There's no school today, Auntie Brenda," I said. "It's still holidays."

"I know, but I've got to tell you something." She sniffed

loudly, wiped her nose with the back of her hand. "It's Pop, Suzette. He's, he's like, passed on." She covered her face with her hands and cried.

I lay there, listening to her. Even though I was nearly ten, I didn't know that passing on was any different than passing out. But the way Auntie Brenda was making such a fuss, I thought that it must be a lot more serious for a man to pass out.

But of course everything to do with men was more serious. I learned that from listening to the kitchen talks, too.

The funeral was a few days later. Gram was in a pretty bad way; she wouldn't come downstairs except to sit at the kitchen table and do a lot of sighing and shaking her head and talking to herself. Auntie Brenda wasn't much good either, spending most of the time out with her boyfriend Len, even though Mom asked her to stay around.

So on Tuesday, before we went to the church, I had to help Mom get everything ready for afterwards. When she went to get Gram dressed, she told me to put the flowers in a vase. They were white and yellow daisies, in a long florist box, from Uncle Vern in Timmins.

"That's lovely, Suzette," Mom said, when she came back. "You did it just right, putting the greenery around the outside. I always did like the look of daisies."

"What other flowers do you like?" I felt the smoothness of one of the yellow petals between my fingers.

"I don't know. Roses, I guess."

"Lilacs?"

She shrugged, moving the sugar bowl a few inches on the tablecloth. "I suppose. They're alright, in a pinch."

"Why didn't you have roses for your wedding?"

"I don't know." Mom gave the wax paper over a plate of lemon tarts a twitch. "Maybe I'm not the kind of person who gets roses. Now go and help Gram down."

As I started up the stairs, she called after me. "Suzette?"
I stopped. I could hardly hear her voice from the
kitchen.
"What made you ask about lilacs?"
I pretended I didn't hear, and ran up the rest of the way.

The winter was long and sad. Pop had never made any
noise, never even said anything, but with him gone the
house was different. Quieter.
    One day in spring, when even the clumps of snow along
the side of the fence had finally melted, I was out on the
back step, helping Auntie Brenda hang up the wet clothes.
There was one of those cold April winds blowing. Auntie
Brenda was supposed to be doing the clothes herself, but
Gram was sleeping again, and Mom had signed up for an
extra Saturday afternoon shift taking tickets at the Deluxe,
so Auntie Brenda knew there was no one to stick up for me.
She made me take the clothes out of the basket and give
them a shake and then hand them to her, and she spread
them on the line and put the clothespins on. In a few
minutes my hands were red and numb.
    "I'm gonna get some mitts," I said.
    "You can't handle clothes with mitts on, dummy." The
clothespin in Auntie Brenda's mouth bobbed up and down.
    "But my hands are freezing. You try digging around in
the basket."
    "Big baby," she said, and pushed me out of the way. She
bent over and pulled out a pair of Gram's big underpants,
but as she straightened up, her face went all rubbery, and
she grabbed onto my shoulder. Then she let go and felt for
the railing and sat down, hard, on the top step. She put her
forehead on her knees.
    "Auntie Brenda?" I said. "What's wrong, Auntie
Brenda?"
    "Nothin'. Leave me alone." Her voice was muffled by
the wool of her coat.

"Are you passing out, Auntie Brenda? Should I get Gram?"

She lifted her head. Her face was so white that her freckles looked like bright red polka dots. Her lips were the same dull colour as the rest of her face, even though I'd seen her put on her new Kiss Me Pink lipstick just before we started the clothes.

"Just shut up, O.K., Suzette? I didn't pass out. I just felt sick for a minute."

"Have you got the flu?"

Auntie Brenda got up, slowly, Gram's underpants still crumpled in her hand. She gave them one little shake, then laid them over the line. She smoothed them down, then her hands fell to her sides and she stood there for a few seconds. I reached up in front of her and put a clothespin at one end of the underpants. The other end started to lift and curl in the wind, but Auntie Brenda just kept standing there, watching it flapping.

"You finish, Suzette," she said, just when I was about to poke her, get her moving again. She opened the back door. "And don't tell nobody I felt sick. Don't tell nobody," she repeated, "or you'll get it."

A few weeks later I heard Mom and Auntie Brenda fighting. They weren't yelling, but their voices had this hard sound that woke me up. Gram wasn't with them; she didn't come down to the kitchen in the evening anymore.

"Don't you realize what you're letting yourself in for?" Mom said, her voice higher than usual. "Only last month you came home crying because he slapped you, after that dance at the legion."

"He just had too much to drink, is all. And he didn't like me dancing with Al Turner."

"Seems to me Len has too much to drink a lot of the time. Brenda, think about it."

"I've thought about it, Win," Auntie Brenda said, her

76

voice all smart. "I'm eighteen. Nobody can tell me what to
do no more."

I heard Mom make a tsking noise, then the creaking
sound of the ironing board being lowered.

"Besides, Win, you're a one to talk. Doesn't appear like
you made such good choices with your life."

There was silence, then the beginning of a thin scream.
"Kettle's boiled," Mom said. "You taking up her tea or me?"

"I'll do it," Auntie Brenda said, but with a sulk in the
words. "Better than staying down here and listenin' to you."

I squeezed my eyes shut when she came through the
living room a minute later. Auntie Brenda's footsteps were
heavy and careful, but I could hear the cup rattling in the
saucer.

The next morning before school I was in my mom's room,
sitting on the window sill watching her get dressed for
work, when Auntie Brenda came in from the bathroom.

"Get out," she said to me.

"I don't have to. Do I, Mom?"

My mother didn't say anything, just lowered herself
onto to the bed. She slipped her foot into one brown leather
shoe, then sat, holding the other in her hands.

"But why, Brenda?" she asked. "After all you've said
about him, complained about, why go and marry him?" It
was like last night's conversation hadn't ended.

Brenda crossed her arms over her chest, gave me a dirty
look. "I thought I told you to get lost, kid," she said.

"Leave her," my mother said, in a low voice that scared
me. I stayed as still as I could.

Auntie Brenda sat down beside my mom. "He's not so
bad, really, Win," she said. "He can be sweet, if he wants
to." She picked at the bottom button of her cardigan,
looking down at it. "Once we get married, I know he'll be
O.K., quit drinking so much. He just needs someone to look
after him."

Mom rubbed her thumb over the scuffed toe of her shoe. "You doing it to get away from here?" she asked. She rubbed and rubbed the shoe, like she could bring back the shine, even though the leather was worn clean away. "Or is there another reason?"

"I got enough saved for a new dress," Auntie Brenda said. "And Len's sister Jacqueline's gonna lend me her shoes, the satin ones she wore when she was a bridesmaid last summer." She kept looking down at the button, just a small clear turquoise button, like there was something about it she'd never noticed before. Then she lifted her head, looked right into my mom's eyes. "And it's a good thing the lilacs will be out. I plan to carry lilacs, like you."

I glanced out the window at the lilac bush, then heard my mom say "Oh Brenda," in a tired kind of voice. I turned to watch her put her arms around Auntie Brenda.

Auntie Brenda started crying, but it wasn't her usual. This time she was just making quiet little breathy sounds, her shoulders shaking. She put her head on Mom's shoulder, and they sat there on the bed, with their arms around each other, rocking back and forth like they were dancing to slow music.

I looked back through the window, thinking about the lilacs with their tight brown buds. Soon they would open into swaying cones of mauve stars, sending their smell in through the screens at night in tiny bursts, too sweet, overpowering.

GONE

"STOP IT, O.K.?"

"Stop what?"

"Humming. It bugs me."

"I wasn't humming."

"Yes you were."

Diana turned her head and looked out the car window. He was doing it more and more lately, the humming. And it never varied. There was no tune, just a steady drone. Usually Diana didn't know how long it had been going on before she noticed it, but eventually she realized she was listening to it with the same mild irritation as when she heard distant nocturnal barking, the dryer murmuring in the basement. Or the purr and click of the concrete under the Volvo's wheels as they sped towards home.

The Saskatchewan prairie stretched out on either side of them, the drained summer sky pushing down relentlessly on the already flattened horizon, the endless mousetail of the highway ahead.

Now there was only silence in the space between them

on the front seat. Diana kept staring out the window, thinking about a woman she'd worked with once, maybe five years ago. The woman had a German accent, was wide-hipped, and her breath came in short, heavy bursts between sentences.

She'd told Diana that every summer she and her husband went driving on their holidays. Got in the car and drove, some years across provinces, other years through states. And the whole time they drove they sang. They brought along songbooks and sheet music, and they argued over whether they'd sing Gilbert and Sullivan or Puccini or the Beatles. They drove their two weeks away, harmonizing within the air-conditioned coolness of their station wagon.

Diana glanced over at Mark, trying to imagine singing with him, but immediately realized it was too intimate, at least now.

"Mark. Do you find yourself thinking about him?"

"Who?"

"Who?" Diana exhaled through her nose. "My father. Who else? We just came from his funeral. God, Mark, who do you think I would be talking about?"

In the lull, Diana felt the beginnings of unspeakable fury, wondering what she'd do if the humming started again.

"I didn't know him, Diana. I only met him once, but like you told me, that wasn't really him. And you never wanted to talk about him, tell me what he was like. Before." He looked over at her. "Like it was some little secret, or something. The Dad I used to know." His eyes went back to the road. "The man no one could live up to." His index fingers beat out a rhythm on the steering wheel. "So it's pretty hard for me to put on this mourning thing now, to pretend I'm broken up."

Diana looked back out through the window at the blurred amber of the fields unfolding. Each mile was so like the one before it that she could pretend they weren't really moving, weren't going forward.

She thought about what Mark had said. It was too hard

to find the right words to describe someone who wasn't there anymore. Wasn't inside a shuffling body, wasn't behind an expressionless face changed only by an occasional puzzled shadow. Someone who was gone.

"Where do you think it all goes?" she said, leaning her head against the window so that her lips touched the glass. "All the memories, all the knowledge? Is it still there, but somehow hidden?" She watched the fog of her breath on the window. "Or, bit by bit, does all the stuff that's been stored over a lifetime fly up and away, out somehow, through the ears and nose and mouth, or even the pores of the scalp, fly away like microscopic insects, looking for freedom? What do you think, Mark?"

She heard Mark put on his signal, knew without looking that he was glancing into the rearview mirror and then shoulder checking. The car swayed slightly as he pulled out from behind the Rolly's Transfer truck and moved up beside it, accelerating steadily and smoothly, finally passing it. The signal clicked on again, and then the car was eased back into the lane, well ahead of the huge turquoise truck. Diana waited, pushing her front top and bottom teeth together in tiny, snipping bites, watching the truck's massive wheels rolling by, concentrating on the pressure of her teeth so that she wouldn't let anything through them. Any words of impatience, sighs of exasperation, while she waited for Mark to answer.

"You know it's not anything like that, Di. It's a type of circuit bypass, simple." Mark used his teacher's voice, his fifth-grade voice explaining long division for the twentieth time.

Diana gave a few more bites, counted them, one, two, three. "I know all the medical theories, how the brain deteriorates." She concentrated on keeping her own voice light, almost nonchalant. "But do you think it's sort of like feeling pain in a missing limb? Except the opposite. All the things the person used to feel. All the missing feelings. Where are they?"

Mark didn't answer. Diana took her lips away from the window, and in the cloud on the glass printed the word WHERE? with her finger. Then, with one quick swipe of her palm, wiped it away.

After they checked into the motel, Diana went back to the car. She opened the trunk and took out a Jim Beam cardboard box, carried it into the room and set it on the desk beside the television.

Mark was lying on the bed, reading the television guide from the top of the TV. He looked up at the thump of the box.

"What's that?"

"Some of my old stuff. My mother gave it to me. She and Lois want to get the attic cleaned out." Her older sister Lois and her husband, Don, lived on the family farm. Don had taken over the farming, and Lois helped her mother run the house and look after their dad. "She wanted me to take my sewing machine, too, but I knew we wouldn't have room in the car. I told Lois to sell it, or give it to someone."

"There's an oldies station here. *Perry Mason*'s on at nine o'clock, then *The Invisible Man* at ten."

Diana opened the box, reached in and pulled out a flat book. "My grade twelve yearbook. God." She put it down on the table and rummaged through the box. "You wouldn't believe the junk that's in here. Look at this." She pulled out a tiny fur hat with a raccoon tail. "Remember Davy Crockett? When I was three or four, my brother got one, and then apparently I made such a fuss about wanting one too that the next weekend my dad drove all the way down into Saskatoon to get me one. Two hours there, two back." She stroked the fur, forward, then the wrong way, watching it bristle. "I can't believe my mother kept all this."

Mark glanced over at it. "Cute. That thing must be a classic by now. You should save it. For our kid." He looked down at the television's remote control, then up at her, running his fingers over the small square buttons like he was reading Braille.

Diana shoved the hat into the box. She turned her back and started to fold the cardboard flaps together. "Probably all moth-eaten, anyway. My mother should have wrapped it up better. She never looked after anything properly. She had all this neat stuff, from my grandmother, things Grandma brought from England, but she let everything get broken, or lost." She heard her own voice, high, the words running together, too fast. She kept working the flaps of the box, jamming one under the other as if the creased cardboard had to close perfectly, folded and unfolded until she heard a click and then the loud canned laughter of a sitcom, and only then, when she felt a sudden release in her shoulders, did she realize how tightly she'd been holding them.

Lying in the bathtub, Diana sipped her Mountain Dew. She put the can on the edge of the tub and ran her fingers up and down the icy moisture on the aluminum sides.

Sounds of *Wheel of Fortune* rattled through the thin wall. There was a long, diminishing whistle that signified a contestant had hit the Bankrupt or Lose a Turn section on the wheel. A perfectly timed groan of disappointment rose from the audience.

Diana closed her eyes. The door opened suddenly, and she sat up, crossing her arms over her chest.

"You scared me," she said, putting her arms down.

Mark smiled. "Who'd you think it would be?"

Diana shrugged. "You just scared me, that's all."

Mark moved the drink can and sat down on the edge of the tub. Diana leaned forward, scooping up the puny wrapped square of motel soap and tearing at the shiny paper. She stopped when Mark reached down and cupped one of her breasts. He ran his thumb across the nipple, watching.

Diana hunched over the soap, fiddling with it, her arms

tight against her body. She felt her front teeth start, the barely perceptible bites, the automatic counting.

Mark took his hand away and stood up, crossing to the counter and picking up the dental floss. Tearing off a piece, he started flossing, leaning against the counter and studying each tooth in the mirror as he worked his way through his mouth. Then he brushed his teeth, slowly, carefully. He rinsed his mouth, patted his lips with the thin white towel.

"You getting out soon?"

"Yeah. In a few minutes."

Mark stood there for an unnecessary second. His eyes moved downward, and Diana fought the urge to bring her arms up in front of her again.

"Hurry up, O.K.?" Mark's voice was soft. Diana closed her eyes and nodded.

When they'd arrived at the farm the day before the funeral, no one was there to meet them except Pablo, an ancient spaniel with a watery bark and cataract-filmed eyes. He was lying in the middle of the gravel driveway, on his side in the dusty shimmer of afternoon August heat. Diana got out of the car and squatted in front of him, holding out her hand and clucking her tongue. "Hey, Pablo. Hi old boy. Remember me?"

Pablo rose stiffly. He yawned silently, then walked unsteadily toward her, his nose raised and quivering. When he got to her fingers he gave a few tentative sniffs and his tail swished twice, politely.

The front door was unlocked, as usual, and Diana went straight to the kitchen, Mark following.

A blue piece of paper was taped on the fridge door. In one corner of the paper there was a shaggy head, open mouth full of sharp teeth emitting a printed roar of words: JUST A LION TO LET YOU KNOW. . . . Following the dots was an explanation from Lois, in her cramped, childish writing. "In town seeing to things. Supper in the fridge if you can't wait. Back by six."

Diana opened the fridge, bent down and peered in. Then she closed the door. "Guess we'll have my old room again," she said, and started toward the stairs.

After they'd brought their bags up, Mark went back outside to wash some of the dust off the car. Diana sat on one of the twin beds, remembering how she and Lois had shared this room until they were both teenagers, until their parents built a new master bedroom downstairs, off the living room, and Lois moved into their old one. Their brother Steven had the smallest room at the end of the hall.

For the last eight years Lois and Don had used the bedroom on the main floor. Diana's room was empty, a guest room, except there were never any guests but her, and her last visit had been over four years ago. Her mother slept back in the old master bedroom, alone, and her father had slept in Steven's narrow room with the sloping ceiling.

From her position on the twin bed, Diana could see the doorway of the little bedroom. The door was open, and the bedspread was smooth and tight, the pillow puffy and undented.

They must have washed the bedding already, Diana thought. She wondered if it had been her mother or Lois who had found him two mornings ago. Were his eyes open or shut? Had he been asleep when he died, or awake, looking at the ceiling and thinking whatever it was he thought about. If anything.

Lois's phone call had been brief. "Dad finally let go, Diana," was all she had said. "The funeral's Saturday."

"We'll leave first thing tomorrow morning," Diana said, "as soon as I let the office know. Did you get hold of Steven?"

"I tried, but there was no answer. And it's a whole day different over there. I'll keep trying, but there's no way, even if I get through to him, that he'll get here in time for the funeral. It's an eighteen-hour flight, I think."

"I know." Diana wrapped the coil of the telephone cord around her middle finger, watched how the skin at the tip of her finger reddened, turned purple. "How's Mum?"

"You know Mum," Lois said.

Now, looking away from her father's bed, Diana stared at the padlock hanging open on the side of the door frame. Don had put the lock on the outside of the room just before Diana's last visit home, saying that since Alf had started roaming at night, it was the only way to keep him safe. Stop him from tumbling down the stairs, from scalding himself in the bathroom, from wandering outside, into the darkness. Her mother had picked at a loose thread around a buttonhole on her sweater the whole time Don was telling Diana about the lock.

On that visit home, when Diana had brought Mark, just after they'd been married, to meet her family, they'd stayed in this room. Diana thought back to their whispering and stifled laughter over the sounds of the groaning bedsprings, trying out first one twin bed, then the other, deciding which was least likely to be incriminating. Then, twice in the night, with her mother sleeping next door, Diana and Mark had stealthy, mummified sex.

After the second time, when Diana lay awake, tracing the curve of Mark's bicep as it rested across her stomach, she heard a sudden frenzied clatter from the locked door down the hall, the doorknob rattling, and a frail voice calling from inside, "Hello. Hello, is anyone there?" Then a rustle and soft padding of feet, her mother's "Shh, shh, Alf, here I am," and the click and turn of a key, the sound of a door quietly opening and closing. Diana gently moved Mark's arm, sitting up and straining to hear.

But all she could make out was the shaky voice, querulous, repetitious, and then her mother's soothing whisper. She listened until she fell asleep, thinking of the times her mother had tiptoed into her room at night, with the same "Shush, I'm here," to lay a warm hand on her forehead and ease her back between the sheets, under the thick quilt, ease her back into safe dreams.

Diana got up and started to unpack their suitcase. She hung up the dress she'd brought for the funeral, Mark's suit. She put her make-up bag on her old desk. She crammed underwear in the empty top dresser drawer, a few tank tops and shorts in the second one. Then she put the oversized T-shirt she wore at night on the twin bed under the window. She took Mark's shaving kit and set it in the middle of the other bed, on the far side of the room.

By the time Lois and Don and her mother got back from town, it was after seven. Diana was shocked at how much older all three of them had grown in the last few years, but kept her face smooth and empty, hugging her mother quickly, not long enough to see if she would be hugged back. Mark nodded and shook Don's hand, patted Lois on the shoulder, and took his mother-in-law's hand and said, "I'm so sorry, Jean," and then, without any warning, dropped her hand and stepped right up to her and put his arms around her, pressing his cheek against her faded hair. Watching, Diana felt a tug of something that was good, and familiar, a letting go somewhere under her ribs. But it slipped away, disappeared, when Don said, "Way past supper," and Mark turned, with too much enthusiasm, Diana thought, from her mother, and looked toward the kitchen.

They all sat at the kitchen table, with plates of potato salad and cold chicken and three-bean combo in front of them, none of them eating except Mark, who had the grace to look ashamed of his appetite, declining second helpings even though Diana knew he was still hungry.

Lois told Diana what would happen at the funeral, who would read the eulogy, which hymns they had chosen, how the few old friends of their father would wear their veterans' uniforms.

And Diana's mother just sat, her hand resting on the table, fingers running up and down the edge of the plastic place mat, looking at a large pyramid of fruit wrapped in crackly cellophane in the centre of the kitchen table, a gift from the Auxiliary Ladies' Group in town.

It wasn't until late the next afternoon, after the funeral, that Diana and her mother were alone.

Lois went to her room to lie down as soon as they got home and carried in flower arrangements and boxes of leftovers from the lunch in the church basement, saying her head was throbbing. Don took Mark out in the pickup to show him something; Diana didn't catch what Don had mumbled as they left. Both Don and Mark had looked guilty, eyes downcast, as they hurried out the back door, away from the silence of the kitchen.

Diana and her mother worked quickly, slicing and dividing leftover ham into meal-sized portions and wrapping untouched casseroles in foil and putting dainties into empty containers.

"I don't know when we'll ever eat all this," Jean said, shaking her head. "I wish some of the others would have taken at least a few of these casseroles back."

Diana mm-hmmed in agreement. The sharp rip and tear of the foil was the only sound until Diana spoke.

"Will you miss him, Mum?" she asked, making a neat silver cover over a square Pyrex container of Maid of Honour Tarts.

Her mother put down the long knife.

"No," she said, "no, I can't say I'll miss him, can't even cry much. I did all that over five years back, when I saw him leaving me, knew I'd lost him." She pulled out another square of foil, tore it with a harsh yank.

"Mark and I can't figure out why you didn't take him into Mariot, over to the seniors' place. Lois told me she'd checked it all out. He would have been O.K. there." She

picked up the Pyrex dish, set it down again, crimping the
foil around the edges, watching her fingers. "I always meant
to come home, Mum, see him again, but, I don't know, I
just . . ." She looked up.

Her mother looked at her, took the kettle off the stove
and turned and filled it at the sink.

Diana spoke to her mother's back. "And it would have
been so much easier for you, Mum. With him in Mariot.
Even with Lois here, I know it's been hard. I know that."

Jean turned on the stove, set the kettle on the element.
She reached into a cupboard overhead and took down a box
of Orange Pekoe, then turned to face Diana again. "Most of
life is hard, Diana. And oftentimes it doesn't much matter
what choice you make, it's still hard. You just have to decide
which of the choices you can live with."

Diana left her mother and the kettle and the table full
of food and went up to the bedroom. She lay down on her
narrow bed with its yellow quilt and matching ruffled
pillow sham, and looked at the other bed, with its
identical bedding, watching the evening darkness creep
across it.

Diana came toward the queen-sized motel bed after her
bath, pulling the elastic out of her ponytail and shaking her
hair down. She smoothed her T-shirt over her thighs. Silent
wrestlers battled it out on the television.

Mark was propped up against two pillows, one hand
making slow circular motions in the dark hair on his bare
chest, the other holding the remote. He looked up at her
and hit the OFF button.

Diana stood, looking down at the bedspread, folded
neatly along the bottom of the bed, the blanket and sheet on
her side pulled down, waiting.

"Mark."

"Hmmm?"

"It doesn't feel right. I mean, my dad just died. It seems

like the wrong thing to do, you know, making love, so . . . soon."

"That's ridiculous, Di. C'mon." He patted the sheet.

She slid in, pulling the blanket up to her chin. "I can't, Mark," she whispered. "I feel strange, like he's . . . I don't know, watching, or something."

Mark switched off the lamp beside him and turned on his side, propping his head up with his hand. "What do you mean, watching? What kind of thing is that to think? And it's the right time, Di. The twenty-sixth and twenty-seventh of this month, right? It's a good thing you're so regular. Come on. Time's a'wastin'." He smiled, leaned close and rubbed under her chin with his nose.

"We can wait till next month."

"We've waited too long already. I figured it out, while we were driving today. It's probably better you didn't get pregnant the last few months. It would have been a winter baby, January or February or March. But if you get pregnant this time, the baby would be born in spring. Perfect. Spring's the best time to have a baby. You can take it outside right away, and by summertime, it'll already be old enough to do things with. We could take it camping, or rent a cabin somewhere."

Diana looked into his eyes. "You've got it all figured out, haven't you?"

"You know I don't mean it like that, Diana. I'm just ready, that's all. I want us to have a baby. I'm ready to be a dad."

He put one leg over her, nudged at her knees with his, smiled. "C'mon." His voice was playful, but there was something else. His knee pushed between hers, harder, and he buried his lips against her neck. "Mommy. Let Daddy in."

Diana's breath caught in her throat. As she turned her head away from Mark, she thought she heard something else, thought she heard the word *please*, but she couldn't be sure, maybe it was just the rustle of the sheet, her own hair swinging against her ear. She looked at the vertical strip of

light on the wall, light from the parking lot, shining
through where the curtains didn't quite meet, and let her
legs unlock.

There was a dull slam of a suitcase lid.

"I've still got a few things to put in, wait," Diana called
through the bathroom door. "I'm just brushing my hair."
She pawed through her make-up bag, and took out a white
plastic bottle that said MIDOL. She quickly unscrewed the
lid and shook a coral-coloured pill out onto her hand, her
saliva already rising. Swallowing the tiny pill, she glanced
down into the bottle. She knew there were exactly fourteen
pills left, half of the twenty-eight she emptied into the
bottle from the plastic wheel she picked up from the
pharmacy each month.

She put the MIDOL bottle back into her make-up bag,
looked at herself in the mirror over the sink, smoothing
down one eyebrow with her ring finger, then zipped up the
bag.

"I just want to stick this in the suitcase," she said, as she
opened the bathroom door.

Mark was sitting on the bed beside the closed suitcase,
in his jeans, the zipper undone, no shirt. Their smaller
nylon bag was still open on the floor.

"Oh. I thought you were ready to go," she said,
surprised to see him sitting, so still.

Mark raised his hands, as if he were going to say
something, then put them on his knees, spreading his
fingers and looking down at them.

"I'm gonna take a quick shower before we head out," he
said.

"Fine. I'll go get some coffee, then. I think I saw a little
coffee shop beside the office. Do you want anything else?"

Mark shook his head and stood up, brushing against her
as he stepped to the bathroom door. She picked up her
purse from the dresser.

"Diana?"

She turned to look at him. He was just standing there, his hands hanging at his sides. "It's not important," he said.

There was a coffee shop, but it was closed. BACK IN TEN MINUTES, said a small, handwritten sign stuck above the door handle. Diana looked at her watch. They could get coffee as they drove out.

She walked back to the unit and let herself in. The bathroom door was closed, the shower running. As she started to lift the Jim Beam box off the desk, planning to put it into the car, she heard a sound from the bathroom. She stood with her fingers curled tightly around the bottom of the box, listening.

Christ, she thought, he's even started to do that humming thing in the shower. Other people sing, he hums. But almost before she finished the thought she realized she was wrong. It wasn't humming, after all.

The sounds were broken, with a jagged, furtive rhythm. As she listened to the muffled noise, Diana knew that Mark was crying, sobbing beneath the harsh bright rattle of the jets of water bouncing against the plastic shower curtain.

She set the box down and walked out of the motel room, back to the coffee shop, leaning against the front window until a tall, harried-looking woman wearing a ragged blue cardigan over a stained uniform with the name Arla embroidered on the breast pocket unlocked the door.

"Only about an hour and a half more. Do you want to stop for lunch, or wait till we get home? Are you hungry?"

Diana shook her head. "Uh-uh. Not really. But there won't be anything to eat at home. I pretty well emptied out the fridge before we left." She looked over at him. "Are you hungry?"

"A little. We can pick up some sandwiches at the deli on Major and eat them at home, though."

"Sure. That sounds good."

Diana kept glancing at him. When she'd got back to the unit with the coffee and two hardening, over-iced cinnamon buns, Mark had been dressed, his wet hair combed straight back. He was crouched over, head down, tying up his runners, but bounced up as she came in, and reached out for the styrofoam cup.

"Great. What's that? Oh, a cinnamon bun. Good. I felt like something sweet this morning."

Diana didn't say anything, fussing with the lid of her own coffee as Mark stirred and stirred his, long after the cream he'd put in had turned the coffee into a smooth mocha.

The last three hours in the car had been quiet. Diana looked through her old yearbook, sometimes nodding and murmuring to herself, sometimes giving little snuffles of surprise.

"I had this dream last night," Mark said. "Remember how we always used to tell each other our dreams? Didn't you even write yours down sometimes?"

"Yeah. For a couple of months. But it got boring."

She thought about her dream. It had startled her awake, sometime in the middle of the night, when everything was motionless and somehow oppressive, no sounds of cars on the highway outside.

Her eyes opened wide in the darkness of the room, and she wondered if she'd spoken, called out loud. But Mark was still a silent mound beside her. It took her a long time to get back to sleep.

"Anyway, this was my dream," Mark said. "I was sitting at a boxing match. The ring was huge, and I was right up at the front. No one was in the ring yet, but I knew it would be a good fight; I was excited about it. And the best thing was that Jack Nicholson was sitting right beside me."

"And?"

"That's pretty well it. I was sitting beside Jack Nicholson at a boxing match. Oh yeah, and he turned to me and said, 'Doncha just love the smella sweat, man?' You know the way he says that, 'man.' He was wearing sunglasses, and he had a cut in his nose. Remember, he got his nostril sliced in that movie, *The China* something, *Syndrome*, or *Connection*, I forget. So his nose had this cut, but it looked all healed, just a pink scar." Mark looked over at her. "Bizarre, eh?" His glance flickered to the road, then back at her. "So what about you, Diana? What did you dream?"

Diana looked into his eyes. She saw the love in them, but it was too big, like something heavy and awkward to carry, something he wouldn't put down. She had to look away.

"Nothing. I guess you did all the dreaming last night." When she felt it was safe, knew he was watching the road again, she glanced at him from the corner of her eye. She saw the broad boniness of his forehead, the earnest thrust of his chin. She knew the way his bottom lip dropped open just the tiniest bit, then closed, every few minutes. That movement of his lip made him look like he was always about to say something. When they first met she kept waiting, wondering what it was he wanted to tell her.

She rubbed her palms over the slightly embossed cover of the yearbook in her lap. The dream was still fresh and clear.

She was walking beside a little boy, and they kept looking at each other and smiling. She knew it was an important day. She took his hand, and it felt warm and comforting in hers. They walked up to a big, red-bricked building, and she bent down and kissed him good-bye, then let go of his hand. Just as he was about to go through the high set of double doors at the front of the building, she saw that it was the wrong place. It wasn't a school, as she first thought, but a meat-packing plant. The little boy looked back at her and waved, and she opened her mouth to call out to him, tell him she'd made a mistake, but he was enclosed and carried off in a rush of men wearing yellow hard-hats and blood-stained white coats.

Diana called his name over and over, although she didn't know what the name was. He didn't hear her, or else couldn't work his way back, through the pushing crowd.

Diana stood outside the doors, helpless, knowing he was gone, and waited, just waited, for something to happen.

LILYROSE

I SWAYED BACK AND FORTH on the old wooden swing, watching Lilyrose run through the sprinkler.

The swing belonged to the landlady who lived on the main floor. In the afternoons, when she was at work, I could use the backyard, but before she got home I had to make sure I was upstairs, with no signs I'd been in the fenced-in scruffy patch of grass. No popsicle wrappers or stray Barbie-doll clothes, no magazine fluttering on the seat of the swing.

The old dragon didn't mind if I put the sprinkler on for Lilyrose on warm days, as long as I wound up the hose when I was done. The afternoon was hot, even for early September, the air heavy and buzzing with heat and insects.

Everything I did was slow, careful, like an invalid just recovering from some long illness. I knew that if I moved too fast something would hurt. I had felt this way on the eighth of September for the last four years. It was the anniversary of the day it had happened, the day Lilyrose had started.

If it had been a boy, I wouldn't have kept him.

I made that clear to the caseworker, told her that I couldn't give her an answer until the baby was born.

Then, I still had to see her before I could be sure of my decision. If she was fair, with his smooth, blond look, I don't know what I would have said.

But when I first held her, and looked down at the tiny head covered with tufts of black hair, and saw the angry, squalling face, the face that reminded me of what was in the mirror in the morning, or late at night, I thought it might be alright.

Lilyrose, I whispered, trying out the name. Lilyrose.

I hoped the name would help, would bring back childhood memories, a rush of love and reassurance. Lily, my mother's name. My grandma Rose. If I started off by naming her after people I'd loved, loving the name, it would naturally lead into loving the child. I thought it would be that easy, the first day.

Lily, right up to the day she died, had been a very earnest woman, not particularly gentle, but strong and calm. A woman who was religious. She didn't have a particular denomination, nothing formal. She had religion itself.

"God's will," she said, about practically anything. It was all God's will. God's will that she had to suffer with arthritis, God's will that we would never have enough money, God's will that men were made the way they were. Until I was nine or ten, I thought that the bad things that happened to my family were a direct result of the curse, this godswill, something unspeakable, mushy and rotten smelling, something to feed to pigs.

I loved my mother in a noisy, roundabout way, pushing

up against her, demanding her time and attention, out-hollering my brothers.

My grandma Rose had heard the calling too, but she talked a lot about the baby in the manger, ignoring my mother's grown-up suffering Jesus. Grandma called me one of His lambs. She sang songs about seeing the little sparrow fall, and shining with a small, clear light.

I loved her in a quiet way that didn't include any touching, but was somehow warm and comforting, like woollen sweaters and pots of homemade soup.

I loved them both, my mother and my grandmother, but in different ways, in the particular way that suited each woman, the way that I knew would let them be comfortable with my love.

So it came as a surprise that I couldn't find the right way to love my daughter. The way that suited both her, and me.

I spied on other mothers at parks and playgrounds. I saw how they wrapped their arms around their children. They whispered into dusty hair and smelled sun-warmed necks and kissed away the hurts on scraped knees and elbows. I wanted to love Lilyrose that way, so whole and unselfconscious, call her honey, sweetheart, even silly things like Babycakes and Angelface. Words that slipped easily, unbidden, from those other mothers. But I couldn't seem to twist my tongue around the words, couldn't make my body soft, open, so Lilyrose could lean into me, like grass into the wind.

I watched Lilyrose squeal and run away from the pulsing needles of water. As she grew bolder, she ran under the arc created just before the sprinkler hit its full height. Braver, she eventually lowered her head over the water, screaming. "Washing my hair, Mommy," she shrieked. "See? Washing my hair."

"That's nice," I said, not wanting to raise my voice, not wanting to jar anything.

After she'd finished with her hair, she stepped one leg over the icy jets and squatted. As the water made its upward journey she laughed, loud and wild. "It's on my pee-pee!"

"Don't do that," I called. "Stop it."

Lilyrose didn't stop, maybe because she heard the annoyance in my voice, maybe because she was getting off on it in some intangible, three-year-old way. Some way that I didn't know about.

"I said stop it," I called again, but she hovered there, suspended easily on her sleek little thighs.

"Why?" she finally yelled.

I looked at her for a second, thinking of a plausible answer. "Because you'll get a cold in your bladder."

She stayed where she was, grinning, staring at me. "What's a bladder?"

I walked over, through the spray, and yanked her arm hard. The grin disappeared. "I said stop it, and I meant it."

Her face screwed up into a square-mouthed, feral look for a second, then she started howling. We stood like that for three up-and-down pulses of the sprinkler. Her screaming while the water beat around me, first up the legs of my shorts, then over my breasts, the icy needles stinging my nipples, and finally biting into my neck and face.

I dropped Lilyrose's arm and made it back to the swing, my legs shaky, head light and unconnected, like I was a kid again, on a carnival ride. The ride that tipped you upside down and held you there until you wanted to spit out the taste of iron, of fear. When you still counted on prayers, and said a silent one: if You don't let me die I'll always be good. I promise.

We came inside just after three. Our apartment was the top floor of the house. The big bedroom was converted into a living room with a strip of kitchen along one side.

The room felt still, dead. I pushed up the window and wedged an old ruler under it. Lilyrose was whining.

"I wanna go back out, Mommy. Play in the water."

"Mommy doesn't feel good, Lilyrose. Why don't you watch TV?"

I turned on the set and adjusted the rabbit ears, twisting the ribbon of foil between them a little tighter. The black-and-white picture jumped and faded, then brightened.

"Look, Lilyrose. *Friendly Giant*. It's just starting."

Lilyrose stared at the television. She stuck out her bottom lip, put her thumb into her mouth.

"Here's the part you like. 'The rocking chair, for those who like to rock.' " I echoed the kindly, patient voice of the TV giant. " 'And the big chair, for two of you to curl up in.' " I looked at Lilyrose. "Which is your favourite chair? The rocker or the big one?"

Lilyrose didn't answer. Her cheeks sucked in and out as she worked on her thumb.

"We'll take off your wet bathing suit, and you can curl up with blankie."

"Soo-soo too," she said, around the thumb.

"Yes. You can have soo-soo."

As I got her into dry clothes and found her blanket and soother, I hoped she'd fall asleep, for just an hour. An hour, that was all I wanted. An hour when I didn't have to talk or listen or nod or smile.

When I could start in on the bag of Oreos in the cupboard, eat them all, if I felt like it. Think about smoking, how good it used to feel to light a cigarette, remembering the pleasure of that first inhale in my chest, that long calming pull. Wait for my heart to slow, numb. So I could sit and imagine the smoke, curling up and away from me, towards the ceiling, snaking across the peeling paint to the lure of the window.

So I didn't have to look into her eyes. Tea-coloured, clear. The same colour as her father's.

I'd only seen his eyes that one night. First on the smoky dance floor, then in his car, the front seat. My head crammed painfully against the door handle, my arms useless, caught under his grinding weight, one knee wedged under the steering wheel, the other held by the crushing grip of his fingers.

His eyes never closed, not even for that final heaving moment. They just flickered once, darkened by the fury that never left them.

I took out the bag of Oreos, set it on the table in front of me, but I didn't open it. On the couch, Lilyrose's head dropped to one side. Her lips parted slightly, and the soother tipped down, no longer caught between her teeth. A wedge of sunlight tripped across the deep chestnut of her hair, picking up golden threads.

I turned off the television and looked back at the cookies, rubbing my thumbnail against my index finger. I put the cookies back in the cupboard, went to the bathroom cabinet and found an emery board and a bottle of polish. Sandy Beach.

I hadn't painted my nails for at least eight months, maybe longer. The polish looked thick, gummy, but when I tried it on the nail of my little finger, it slid on, wet and shiny. The polish made my nail look longer, the finger more graceful. I did my whole left hand.

As I started in on my right, I noticed Lilyrose rolling her head back and forth. In another minute she sat up and the soother dropped, unnoticed, between the cushions.

Lilyrose went to the plastic laundry basket beside the TV, started digging through the jumble of toys. She was so small, so self-absorbed, busily wrapping something in her blankie. I saw her mouth moving, caught the slight hiss of her words as she talked to herself.

102

"What are you playing?"

Lilyrose looked over, startled, as if she'd forgotten I was there. She came to me, cradling the blanket, and pulled aside one corner of the worn material, showing me the lifeless face of a brown monkey.

"Oh. George. Curious George."

"Not George." She carefully folded the blanket back over the monkey's face.

"Because George not a good name for a girl monkey," she said, looking up at me, as if she had heard my silent why, why not George?

Her eyes widened, and before she looked back down again, I saw a soft glimmer so swift, so tiny, I almost missed it. In that second her eyes magnified, looked like a painting that had smeared, then were clear again.

Lilyrose went back to the couch.

I kept on with the sticky brush, the last slow, careful strokes, my left hand unsteady.

"What do you call it, then?" I stared at my hand, fingers spread wide on the table.

"Judith."

At the sound of my name I looked away from my hand, at Lilyrose.

"What?"

"Judith. Monkey's name is Judith." Lilyrose sat on the edge of the couch, holding the wrapped animal against her chest, rocking and humming tunelessly. After a few minutes she gently laid it down beside her.

"Mommy loves you, Judith," she said. "You're a good little snuggle-baby."

I watched her patting the little bundle, murmuring to it, until a shadow fell across the couch, across her gold-lit hair and eyes, and my nails were dry.

ABSOLUTION

SYLVIE WAS THINKING about fingers just before she gave birth to Raymond.

The night the baby was born, when Sylvie was in the labour ward at Precious Blood, she had been reading a new magazine, the April 1953 issue of *Woman at Home*. She needed a distraction, something to help pass the time and hold down her growing panic at the unimagined power of the pain. Although one of the Sisters on the evening shift assured Sylvie that her labour was progressing, it was very slow, Sister said, as is often the case with first babies.

Sylvie was frightened, alone in the darkened ward, hearing the sounds of other women in labour, especially upset by the screaming of the huge woman with a moustache in the bed beside hers. The woman's wailings and shrieks were in a language foreign to Sylvie, but they had a heavy Slavic sound. At times the woman sounded like she was praying, at other times cursing. Sylvie covered her ears with her hands and wept when the woman's cries became unbearable. Eventually two men pushing a stretcher came in, and with a lot of grunting and one loud "merde," hauled the woman onto the gurney and wheeled her out.

Once she was gone Sylvie was able to calm herself, and had gone back to the magazine that the smocked woman with the book cart had left on the foot of her bed earlier that evening. Sylvie didn't feel like reading, but forced herself to flip through the pages, studying the pictures in the dull circle of yellow light from the lamp attached to the wall over her head. At the sound of heavy footsteps approaching the ward, she leaned forward, hoping it was someone with her shot. Her friend Lise, who had her first baby seven months earlier, had told her to hold on until the shot, which meant that soon she would be given an anesthetic to knock her out, and she wouldn't feel it when the baby was actually born.

"They should put you out at the first pain," Lise had said around the large safety pin in her mouth. She shook a generous powdering of cornstarch onto her daughter's bottom. "It's crazy, to make you suffer, eh? When they can make it stop, just like that." She snapped her fingers. "Gives them power, those cold-hearted nurses, to see you begging for mercy. They like it, I tell you. Next time, me, I don't care, I won't try to be brave, like with this one." She gestured with her chin towards the baby as she pulled a pair of rubber pants up over the clean bulky diaper. "I'll scream my head off, so loud they'll want to shut me up."

Sylvie thought she'd have to tell Lise it wouldn't work. The woman in the next bed had screamed for hours, and they hadn't given her anything. One nun after another would appear soundlessly, gliding white shadows, close the curtain around the bed with a practised twitch, and then swish it open, a minute later. Sylvie had heard one of them, the older, tired-looking one, say, her voice sharp, "That's not doing anybody any good, Madame. You have a long way to go." The woman hadn't heard, or hadn't understood, or hadn't cared, and went on bellowing and howling.

Sylvie slumped back against her pillow when the

footsteps kept on going, past the labour ward. No shot yet. She looked down at the magazine, open to an article called "Your Body, Your Destiny." It was a chart, showing what certain physical characteristics could imply. The article mentioned the forehead, eyes, nose, mouth, and ears as clues to the personality within. Sylvie turned to the next page to read about parts of the body, looking for what the article said about fingers.

She had particularly loved Jean-Luc's fingers. As the next wave of pain hit, she closed her eyes, thinking about the times she had picked up one of his thin strong hands and kissed each of the fingertips. She had often marvelled that hands that could bale hay could also create beauty with a paintbrush, could trace the lines of her body with such tenderness.

According to the article, it was splayed fingers that were the sign of a creative person, one possessing an artistic temperament. Sylvie immediately thought of her cousin Alphonse. She remembered his fingers as being definitely splayed, each digit thick and stubby, with the tip bigger than the rest of the finger, and slightly flattened. Alphonse had methodically tortured any barn cat he could get hold of, and did unspeakable things to the large grasshoppers he caught around the pump in the yard. She and her sister had been afraid of him, and made sure they were never alone when Alphonse was out for his regular summer visit. They stuck together for the whole week, going out to the hen house for eggs or down to the dark cellar to bring up a pail of potatoes for supper. And no matter how hot it was, they never went to the dugout for a swim. Not with Alphonse around, following them, spying on them from behind bushes and watching them with his strange, heavy-lidded black eyes, little seeds in puffy, unripened pods.

The last she had heard, Alphonse, now just Al, was serving time for aggravated assault over at Stony Mountain. To her knowledge he had never showed any signs of creativity, except with the grasshoppers.

In the middle of a memory about Alphonse, Sylvie was gripped with such pain she couldn't read anymore, and threw the magazine to the floor, crying and calling for help. A Sister materialized, pulled up Sylvie's gown and gave a quick look and a few pokes, and left. In a minute she returned holding a long needle high in the air, and rolled Sylvie onto her hip. Sylvie felt it sink deep into her flesh. She twisted and moaned as she felt herself being pulled onto a stretcher, like the foreign woman, and she was wheeled down a dark corridor.

She was left in a hallway, outside a pair of swinging doors, and fell into a strange state of dullness. She closed her eyes, felt herself moving. She was aware of very bright lights, even with her eyes closed, and wondered if her mother had finally put a light in the cellar, so she didn't have to put her hand into the potato bin worrying about spiders. She was breathing something, an odour sweet yet sickening, and she knew Alphonse was hurting one of the cats again, one of the new kittens, except it was her he was hurting, and then the kitten was crying, on and on, its wail high and thin, in the insistent, senseless way of kittens. After that she let the dullness grip her more tightly, surrendering to the deep numbing darkness with relief.

She was awakened by a loud voice. "Madame Bertrand. Madame Bertrand. Come. It is time to wake up."

Sylvie's head was turned toward a window beside her bed, and as she fought to drag herself out of the thick fuzz she saw meagre grey light, and realized that it was morning, that it must be over. A soft spring rain was falling soundlessly outside the grimy panes. Sylvie put her hand to her face, to her neck; they were wet with sweat. She tried to lick her lips, her tongue thick and dry as if it were padded with gauze. She heard murmuring voices, babies crying.

She looked up at the nurse, read Sister Therese on the bar pinned on the woman's low white bosom. Sister

Therese plucked a small tightly wrapped form from
between two identical blanketed shapes on the top level of a
wheeled cart. She reached inside the blanket, peered at
something, then picked up Sylvie's limp arm and read the
plastic band around her wrist.

"Your son, Madame Bertrand." Sylvie was aware of the
emphasis placed on the Madame. She reached toward the
blanket.

"Small, this one. Only five pounds, nine ounces," Sister
Therese said, placing the almost weightless bundle in the
crook of Sylvie's right arm.

As Sylvie stared down at the tiny stranger, Sister
Therese continued briskly. "We gave him a bottle at four
this morning. We will bring him to you every four hours
during the day, for you to feed him." She turned to leave.

"Could you open the window, Sister?" Sylvie said. "I
am very hot."

The nurse shook her head, the folds of her veil brushing
her sallow cheeks. "Mais non. Not until the fifteenth of
May. The rules." As she pushed the baby cart to the next
bed, she said over her shoulder, "The instrument marks will
soon fade," then she hurried on, her shoes squeaking
alarmingly on the waxed tiles.

Sylvie waited until the rest of the babies were passed
out. Once the Sister had left the ward, she carefully sat up
and laid the sleeping baby on his back, on top of her legs.
He startled when she unwrapped the tight flannel blanket,
throwing out his arms and legs in alarm, his closed eyes
squeezing together and his mouth opening in silent protest.
But he didn't wake.

Sylvie studied the baby in the grey morning light,
looking for signs of Jean-Luc, but it was hard to come to
any conclusions. She couldn't see his eyes, and his ears were
folded tightly against his head. His nose was no more than a
nub, his lips pursed primly. His forehead was high and
narrow, protruding the smallest fraction just before the soft
fringe of dark hair. She touched the square purple-red

bruise on each temple, wondering if a tiny baby felt the pain
of being pulled out of his snug home.

Suddenly remembering the strange half-dream about
Alphonse, Sylvie quickly lifted the baby's clenched hand,
unfurling the matchstick fingers one by one. She smiled as
she bent her head and kissed the straight, delicate tips.

"You will be an artist, mon petit Raymond," she
whispered, lifting the warm body and putting her lips to the
downy forehead. "You will make Maman proud." She
rubbed her lips back and forth in a feathery motion. "Oui,"
she whispered, "we won't care what anyone says. You will
be my handsome, clever boy, and you will make beautiful
pictures." She moved her lips closer to the baby's curled ear.
"Just like your papa."

Raymond didn't miss his father. He didn't even know that
he was absent, didn't notice that there was anything
different about his small family, just him and his mother, at
least not before he started school. He played quietly in the
living room with his piles of wooden blocks and his little
metal cars and trucks and crayons and old envelopes and
scraps of butcher paper, while his mother stood all day in
the kitchen, cutting and dying and perming the hair of the
ladies of St. Emile.

Sometimes, if he got bored, he wandered into the
kitchen, wrinkling his nose at the strong chemical smell. He
would push a car among the wisps of brown and black and
blond and white hair on the worn linoleum, or stand and
watch his mother wrap a crinkly white square of paper
around a piece of hair and then roll it all up on a long metal
rod and clip it, so quickly Raymond would hardly keep track
of his mother's fingers.

All day, every day, there was a lady in the kitchen,
sitting in the special chair in front of the mirror or reading a
magazine with her head under the huge metal hood. The
radio on top of the fridge was always playing loud, happy

music, over the sound of the running water or the hair dryer. And even if his mother was talking, or her hands were covered in shampoo, or she was snipping away with a pair of sharp scissors, she would smile and stop what she was doing long enough to bend down and kiss Raymond's forehead if he came and stood beside her.

The kitchen had been made into the hair salon by Sylvie's aunt Lucille. Lucille had written just before Sylvie had finished high school, inviting her to come and live with her, learn the trade, and eventually take over the business. Lucille wanted to move out east, to be closer to her children and grandchildren. Sylvie had come on the first bus after graduation, excited at the prospect of a new life in a new place, at the prospect of a future, and glad to get away from the windswept farm and her hard-drinking father and whining stepmother.

One section of the kitchen counter and the cupboard over it had been removed, and a deep sink with a long hose installed. Beside the sink was the big red leather chair that Raymond loved. It could spin around, and if his mother pumped a lever with her foot, it could go up and down. Most evenings, after supper, his mother would put him in the chair and give him rides, up and down, up and down. Raymond would watch himself in the big mirror on the wall in front of the chair, making faces and holding his arms over his head when he went up, then putting them down for the descent.

The first day of school Raymond learned to feel shame.

He was the youngest of the seven children starting grade one. The provincial education laws said that a child must be six by December 31 in order to begin school, but Raymond had just turned five when the principal came to see Sylvie on a warm April day.

The principal had looked around the town for a few more students for the upcoming year; there was a very small crop of grade one students that particular year, and a lot of the older boys, in the eighth grade for the second or third year, had dropped out, bringing attendance numbers down. The principal was worried about the reaction of the district school board. Some of the schools in small towns had been closed in the last few years, the children bussed to larger neighbouring towns. If the school in St. Emile were to close, the principal would be out of a job.

The principal sat in Sylvie's living room. He looked at little Raymond, big-eyed, with his head of dark shining curls.

"He would enjoy being with the other children in grade one in September," he said. "He must get lonely, on his own here."

Sylvie looked down at Raymond, colouring on a brown paper bag at her feet.

"He looks like a very bright boy," the principal said.

Sylvie brushed Raymond's hair back from his forehead. Raymond looked up at her. "Yes. He learns very quickly."

"Good, then. He'll be fine. It's settled." The man slapped his hands on his knees, signalling the end of the visit.

Sylvie bit her bottom lip. "It's just that I had hoped, well, there has been talk of a new lower-grade teacher for the last two years. After all, it is common knowledge that Madame Painchaud is expected to retire very soon, and, well," she stopped, and the principal saw a tiny bead of blood on Sylvie's full bottom lip—"you know how it stands. . . ."

The principal got to his feet. "There are no staff changes indicated for the next year, or the one after that, at this point. Legally Madame Painchaud has three years until retirement. She has been a teacher in St. Emile for such a long time, for almost forty years, the records show, and there has never been a formal complaint." He studied Sylvie's hands, still caressing the boy's smooth forehead. "I understand your concern, Mademoiselle Bertrand, but we are all adults, are we not? We must go forward with our lives, and not dwell on the past."

Sylvie nodded, still biting at her lip as she closed the door behind the principal. Later, when Raymond asked for a ride in the chair, she said "No!" sharply, and told Raymond to put on his pyjamas and go to bed.

Surprised, Raymond silently did what he was told. Just as he was falling asleep, he felt his mother tucking the blanket over his shoulders, smelled her good familiar smell of shampoo and hairspray as she kissed his cheek, and he knew everything was alright again.

After everyone had been assigned their seats the first day of school, the grade one to four teacher, Madame Painchaud, asked each child to stand up and state their full name, age, then the name of their mother and father.

"The class lists must be checked," she said, opening a folder on the top of her desk. She adjusted the thick glasses on her nose, and picked up a long pointy stick with slow, stiff movements. "Marc will demonstrate for us." She waved the stick at a boy in the back of the grade four section.

Raymond turned in his seat. Since he was smallest, he had to sit in one of the desks in the first row, right in front of the teacher. He watched the tall boy get to his feet and chant, "Marc Charbonneau, age nine. Papa, Henri Charbonneau. Mama, Yvette Charbonneau."

Madame Painchaud smiled tightly. "Well done. Now, the rest of you please, starting with the grade fours, then the grade threes, twos, and finally, our new grade one students."

Raymond watched and listened with interest. He saw that every time a student spoke, Madame Painchaud nodded and marked something on the paper in front of her on her desk.

Halfway through the grade twos, Raymond realized three things. That many of the children had the same last name, some even had the same mama and papa. That nobody had the same last name as his. And that he didn't have a papa.

He got a bad heavy feeling low in his stomach. He tried not to think about it. Finally it was his turn. He stood up.

"Raymond Bertrand. Age five. Mama, Sylvie Bertrand."

He sat down, looking at the scarred top of his wooden desk. There was a sharp knocking noise. He looked up. Madame Painchaud was tapping the edge of her desk with her stick.

"I don't believe you are finished, Raymond. Stand."

Raymond stood up again.

"Did you not hear the other children, Raymond?"

Raymond nodded.

"We do not nod. We answer, yes, Madame Painchaud, or no, Madame Painchaud."

Raymond kept his head down. "Yes, Madame Painchaud."

"Yes, yes what? What are you saying yes to, Raymond? And look up."

Raymond slowly raised his eyes.

"Speak, Raymond. Did you hear the other children?"

"Yes, Madame Painchaud."

"And?"

Raymond fixed his eyes on the pointy stick. He jumped when Madame Painchaud tapped the side of her desk with it, harder than before.

"And, Raymond, you stated your name, good, your age, good, and your mother's name. But you did not tell the class the name of your father."

The room was still, and hot. Raymond stared at the pointer; it grew too bright, and there was a buzzing noise, far off, from the back of his head.

"Who is your papa, Raymond?"

Raymond opened his mouth, but no sound came out. He tried again. "I don't know." It was a whisper.

"Pardon, Raymond? Did you say you don't know? You don't know? But of course you know. Everyone has a papa, Raymond."

There were a few stifled giggles in the room.

"Certainly your mama has told you about your papa."
Raymond was afraid to look at her. Her voice was loud and
there was something in it that made the heaviness in
Raymond's stomach hurt even more.

"It is not nice to keep secrets, Raymond. It is not fair to
the other children. Children, how many of you know the
name of Raymond's papa?"

Raymond heard rustling noises, the scraping of feet. He
couldn't take his eyes off the pointer, but even looking
straight ahead he could see a few arms waving in the air on
either side of him, colourful graceful stalks in plaids and
printed cotton, the hands on the ends proud white blossoms.

Madame Painchaud looked down at the paper on her
desk, read from it. "Raymond Bertrand. Age five. Mother,
Sylvie Bertrand. Father . . ." She hesitated, then looked up
from the paper, stared at Raymond. "Father, Jean-Luc
Painchaud. Now sit down."

When Raymond sat down, he realized he had wet his
pants.

Raymond's first report card, in early November, was full of
black crosses. He sat in the red leather chair, looking at his
mother's reflection in the mirror. Sylvie sat behind him at
the kitchen table, reading the sectioned paper. Raymond
scratched at the back of his hands, at the rash that had
itched and burned since the middle of September.

"What does it say, Maman?" Raymond finally asked,
after Sylvie had carefully re-folded the paper and slid it back
into its narrow envelope.

"Well, Raymond, it says that you are not listening well.
And because you don't listen, you have trouble
understanding what you are to do. You don't finish your
work. Is it true? That you don't listen to . . . to the teacher?"

Raymond looked at the tiny scabs covering the back of
his hands. He picked one off, looking at the fresh pink skin
underneath.

"I listen, Maman. But she doesn't look at me, or talk to me. If I put up my hand, she doesn't call on me. She doesn't put my pictures on the wall with the others." He squeezed the scab between his fingers. "Maybe she doesn't like me, Maman. Why doesn't she, Maman? I try to be a good boy."

Sylvie got up and came over to the red leather chair. She took a jar from the shelf under the mirror, and scooped a blob of soft white lotion out with her fingers. She picked up Raymond's hand and began to gently smooth it onto the scaly skin. When she had done both hands she put the jar back and began to pump the chair, up and down, until a thin smile appeared on Raymond's lips.

As Sylvie walked to the front door of the school, a sudden gust of cold, dry air brought a few blackened leaves rattling up the bare concrete in front of her. She smelled snow. It was late this year.

She went to the principal's office. The door was ajar; as she knocked it swung open. The principal was standing in front of an open filing cabinet.

"Oh! Mademoiselle Bertrand," he said, looking up from the folder he held in his hand. "Can I help you?"

"I'd like to see Madame Painchaud, please, Monsieur Lussier."

The principal glanced at his watch. "I believe she would be in the workroom at this time. She always prepares her next day's work immediately after dismissal."

"Should I go to the workroom?"

"Oh, no, you can meet here, if you like." He gestured to the small round table in one corner of his room. Three chairs sat around the table. "Please, have a seat," he said.

Sylvie looked at the chairs. "No. I would rather speak to her alone, please. Perhaps in her classroom."

"Yes, that would be fine, Mademoiselle. If you would go down the hall, and wait for her in her room, I will send her to you."

Sylvie nodded and started out the door.

116

"Is there a problem, Mademoiselle Bertrand?" the principal said.

Sylvie turned her head and looked at him over her shoulder, but didn't answer.

The classroom was spotless, but had a dusty, rubbery smell. Green cloth blinds were pulled exactly halfway down on the four windows along one wall, giving the room a sleepy look. The daylight was already fading, but it was too early to have the lights on. As the radiator gave a hissing squeal, Sylvie shivered.

She looked around the classroom. A pitted blackboard ran behind the large metal desk at the front of the room. The young Queen Elizabeth stared vacantly, unsmiling, from an ornate gilt frame over the blackboard. The wall at the back of the room had a bulletin board divided into four sections, one for each of the grades.

Sylvie walked over to the bulletin board and studied the grade one section. There were six pictures thumbtacked on the cracked board. There wasn't one with Raymond's name on it.

She turned at the creak of a footstep on the wooden floor. Madame Painchaud was standing in the doorway, under the large wooden crucifix, a pile of mimeographed papers in one hand. The two women stared at each other for a fraction of a second, then the older one walked to her desk, her black laced shoes thumping with each step. She put the papers down on the top of her desk and looked at Sylvie.

"You wished to see me?"

Sylvie walked toward her. She stopped at the small desk just in front of the teacher's.

"Is this Raymond's desk?" she asked.

Madame Painchaud nodded.

"Yes. He told me he sits right in front of you. Because he is the smallest, you told him."

"That is correct."

Sylvie took a breath. "Madame Painchaud, I came to see you because of Raymond's report, because of the things you wrote. I cannot believe Raymond is performing so miserably in every area. I know my son. He is not a dull boy. He is young, yes, but he is clever."

"Being clever does not necessarily ensure good grades."

"Madame Painchaud. Raymond tells me that you don't help him, that you don't talk to him, except to tell him his work is wrong, is careless. But he is only a small boy; perhaps he is confused about something, misunderstands. I have come to hear your side."

"My side? *My* side? I do not have to answer to a parent about my side. I am the teacher. I answer only to Monsieur Lussier."

Sylvie took a step closer. "Madame. Please. We are talking about a five-year-old boy who cries in the morning because he is afraid to come to school, who has started to wet the bed, who has developed a rash on his hands and arms."

"These things are not uncommon with children, Mademoiselle. You do not know children the way I do. I have dealt with children my whole life. These things come and go. They mean nothing."

Sylvie's voice was so low the grey-haired woman had to lean forward to hear. "We are talking about your grandson, Madame."

The older woman's nostrils flared briefly. "I prefer not to be reminded. It is shameful. Every day I must face . . . him, with everyone looking, everyone knowing, that he is a product of sin. You should have left town, Mademoiselle Bertrand, when Jean-Luc, after the accident, when Jean-Luc," She stopped for a moment. "When Jean-Luc died. You should have run away, hidden your shame. But no, you stayed, stayed on for everyone to see your condition, to know how you had led my son astray. Then you had the nerve to keep the child, go on as if everything was normal. It is despicable."

"Perhaps you, and some others, Madame Painchaud, do not like what has happened. After his first day here, I realized I had made a mistake by not explaining things to Raymond. When he came home crying, with questions, I tried to talk to him, tell him the situation in simple terms. But he cannot grasp it. He only knows now that you are his mamère, yet you do not act like the other grandmothers he sees at the homes of his friends." She stopped, ran her fingers over the gouges on the top of the desk. "I had hoped, in time, that you, you might . . ." She looked up at Madame Painchaud's face. What she saw made her drop her eyes again.

"It's not his fault, Madame Painchaud, it's not Raymond's fault, who he is. You cannot blame the child."

"I do not assign blame. That is God's work."

Sylvie watched her own fingers tracing the scratches on the wood. "I do not believe that God blames or judges, Madame Painchaud. And I don't believe God would wish you to punish a child for his mother and father's—"

"Since you are so willing to inform me, Mademoiselle," the woman interrupted, "of how God would wish me to act, perhaps you are forgetting that the child will have no place in heaven. That fact can never change. The boy cannot be baptized, born outside the sanctity of marriage. A bastard!"

Sylvie looked up in time to see droplets fly from the older woman's lips as she spit out the last clipped word.

"He is a child of love, Madame Painchaud. You know Jean-Luc and I planned to marry. Everyone knew that. We planned it long before Raymond was conceived. The date was set for as soon as the crop was harvested. We had arranged for the church, and Jean-Luc had spoken to Father Archambeault about the banns. Jean-Luc said—"

"Stop!" Madame Painchaud's lips were a thin white line. "Don't speak his name to me. You say it as a caress. It sickens me. Do you hear? It sickens me. *You* sicken me. Whore!"

The word slammed across the three-foot distance

119

between the women. Sylvie felt for the seat of Raymond's desk, and lowered herself onto it.

In the silence, Sylvie could hear Madame Painchaud's heavy breathing, saw her hollow chest rise and fall. The woman placed her gnarled hand against the starched white frills of her blouse.

"He was a saint, my Jean-Luc." The voice had lost its shrillness, was quiet, almost a reverent whisper. "He was a dutiful son. Pure, clean. Until you came along, tossing your long curls, wearing fancy clothes, even during the week. You tempted him, dirtied him. He talked of the priesthood, my Jean-Luc, would have taken his vows, if it weren't for your arrival in town. All the boys swarmed around you, like flies. You could have had your pick, but you chose the only one you couldn't have. The one who had promised himself to God."

Sylvie pushed herself out of the small seat, crossed her arms over her chest. "I'm sorry, Madame. That is not so. That was your dream for Jean-Luc. Not his. He never wanted to be a priest, no matter how you tried to persuade him. He wanted only to paint."

Madame Painchaud stared into Sylvie's eyes.

"I have all of his paintings, Madame. Did you know that? Did you wonder what happened to them? He brought them to my aunt's house, when you threatened to destroy them. He had a talent, Madame. A real talent. And now his son, your grandson, has that talent. You see in Raymond the very thing you couldn't accept in Jean-Luc. And now you are trying to punish Jean-Luc, and me, by punishing a little boy, my little boy. And I cannot let you do that, Madame."

Madame Painchaud's chin quivered, once. She turned her back and started to savagely brush the already clean blackboard.

"Get out," she said, her voice strange, guttural. "Go."

Sylvie opened the top of Raymond's desk. She took out his printing notebook, his scrapbook, a little primer, and a thick pencil with a chewed end. She quietly closed the top of the desk and, clutching Raymond's things against her chest, walked out of the classroom, leaving Madame Painchaud still scrubbing at the blackboard.

Raymond handed his mother the ornaments, watching as she attached each one to a branch of the small pine in a corner of the living room.

"How long, Maman, how long is it now?"

Sylvie looped the thread of the red-and-white striped ball over a high branch. "Still one week, Raymond. The same as this morning. Seven days." She held out her hand for the last ornament, a plastic dove. "You've finished your printing lesson?"

Raymond's forehead creased. "Almost."

"Almost?"

"Only two more lines of Rs. But I already know R. I know how to make all the letters. Why do I have to keep printing? Madame Painchaud never made the grade ones do eight lines of each letter. Only five. I want to draw something. It's Friday afternoon. Friday afternoon was art time."

Sylvie clipped the bird to the branch. "I have an idea, a way you can practise your letters and draw at the same time. You can make Christmas cards for your friends. Now go, go and get your crayons."

Sylvie went to a drawer in the small telephone table and took out a box containing a pad of stiff paper and matching envelopes. She brought it to the coffee table, where Raymond was kneeling, with his crayons neatly lined up in front of him.

Sylvie crouched down beside him. "Now, I will fold each paper in half, like this. On the front you can make a beautiful picture, anything you like, and I'll show you how to spell Merry Christmas. You can copy it inside, and print your name underneath. How many cards do you think you will make?"

She waited while Raymond whispered to himself, looking at his fingers. "Eight," he said. "I will make eight cards."

Sylvie folded eight squares of paper, printed JOYEUX NOËL in block letters on the cover of the writing pad, then went to mix up a batch of Black as Night colour for Madame Fouchard, her three o'clock appointment. She left Raymond staring at the row of unframed paintings on the wall across from the coffee table.

Raymond finished his cards just as Madame Fouchard left.

"Can I use the envelopes, too, Maman?" he asked, coming to the kitchen holding the folded papers.

"Envelopes?"

"Yes. Tomorrow morning, we will go to the post office and give the cards to Monsieur Ayott, and he can put them in the little boxes. All the mail in the little boxes is in envelopes."

Sylvie threw the dustpan of hair into the garbage bin and put the broom and dustpan in the corner behind the back door.

"Yes, you can use the envelopes. Do you know how to spell your friends' names?"

Raymond nodded. "All except Solange."

"I'll show you. But can I look at your cards?" She walked towards Raymond, smiling. "You must have worked very hard on them, spending all this time."

The boy pressed them against his sweater. "No. It will spoil the surprise."

Sylvie clapped her hands together. "A surprise?"

"Yes. I made one for you too. But you can't see it yet. You will have to wait until Monday, and pick it up from Monsieur Ayott." Raymond started back to the living room, to begin the envelopes. "Everyone will have to wait until Monday," he announced solemnly.

At ten o'clock on Monday night, Sylvie was in her
housecoat, boiling water for tea. There was a knock on the
front door. Sylvie glanced at the clock, a furrow appearing
between her eyebrows. She turned off the element under
the kettle and pulled the front of her flannel robe closer
around her neck. Crossing the darkened living room, she
stopped to switch on the floor lamp beside the couch.

When she snapped on the outside porch light, Madame
Painchaud's face was illuminated in the diamond of glass in
the door. A woollen scarf, coated in snow, covered her grey
crown of braids.

Sylvie opened the door, letting in a gust of snow.

"May I come in?"

Sylvie stepped back, opening the door wider. As the
older woman started across the threshold, she stopped, her
mouth opening as she looked at the wall facing her.

"Please, I cannot close the door," Sylvie said. The
woman didn't move. Sylvie took her by the coat sleeve and
pulled slightly, so that the woman moved forward, and
Sylvie was able to shut the door against the frigid air.

They stood in silence. Madame Painchaud's eyes moved
from painting to painting, stopped on one.

"Madame?" Sylvie finally said.

Madame Painchaud closed her mouth, blinked once,
twice. She turned to Sylvie. Her eyes were swollen, her skin
an unnatural waxy texture.

Sylvie motioned to the couch. "Perhaps you should sit
down. Are you unwell?"

The skin under Madame Painchaud's left eye rippled.
Sylvie noticed she was holding a large, creased brown
envelope under one arm.

"Yes," Madame Painchaud said. "I will take a seat."

Sylvie followed the woman to the couch. She saw that
Madame Painchaud had forgotten to put her boots on, and
her shoes and heavy lisle stockings were wet. Sylvie

suddenly thought of her own mother, so long ago, before she was sick and worn out from hard work, before she died, and felt a rush of sadness, an unexpected surge of pity for Madame Painchaud.

"I am just making a pot of tea. Would you like a cup?"

Madame Painchaud didn't seem to hear her. "I came to see Raymond," she said, still looking at one of the canvases.

"But it is very late, Madame. He has been in bed for some time."

Madame Painchaud put the brown envelope on the coffee table, reached up and pulled the scarf off her head. "Oh. Yes. Of course. A little boy would be in bed." Then she leaned forward, reaching inside the brown envelope. "I came to thank him," she said, pulling out a familiar rectangle. "For my card." She held the envelope toward Sylvie. "Have you seen it?"

Sylvie took it, shaking her head. On the front, MME. PAINCHAUD was printed in round, sloping letters. The C was backwards. Sylvie looked at it for a long time. "I didn't know. He made some cards, for his friends, he said, and one for me, and he gave them to Monsieur Ayott. I picked up mine today, too."

She looked toward the window sill. In the middle of a row of brightly coloured commercial cards sat the folded paper, decorated with a baby in a bed of yellow and brown. Over the baby's head was a round yellow circle. A smiling animal stood beside the baby; it could have been a cow or a horse.

Sylvie looked at Madame Painchaud's envelope again, then pulled out the card.

On the front was a woman. She was dressed in blue, a blue dress, blue hat, darker blue shoes. She held the hand of a little boy. The boy had light brown curly hair, a red shirt, and overalls. He looked up at the woman, and she looked down at him. They were both smiling. Behind them was a bright blue vase. Tall spikes of purple burst from the narrow neck of the vase. At the bottom were a jumble of small black letters, but they didn't spell anything. She opened the card. In red and green crayon, Raymond had printed TO MAMÈRE JOYEUX NOËL RAYMOND.

Sylvie raised her head and looked at the painting Madame Painchaud was still looking at. It was a sophisticated version of Raymond's card. In the lower right-hand corner, in Jean-Luc's neat hand, were his initials, and one word, Absolution.

Madame Painchaud reached inside the brown envelope again, and this time took out a paper, painted with water colours. It was a picture, almost identical to Raymond's. A boy holding a woman's hand. The blue vase, purple flowers.

"Jean-Luc painted it for me when he was six or seven. Do you know the story behind it?"

Sylvie pushed a strand of hair that had fallen across her face behind one ear, and looked at the painting on the wall.

"Jean-Luc told me something about it. That he had broken your favourite vase, and had been scared to tell you. But when you found out, you weren't mad after all."

An unfamiliar softness on her face erased some of the lines etched down Madame Painchaud's cheeks. "It was a vase, a blue vase, that my grandmother had given me. I always used it in the spring, when the irises came out. The colours of the flowers were so perfect in the vase. One May, when the irises opened, I looked for my vase. But it wasn't in the cupboard, where I always kept it. Later that month, putting away some blankets, I found the broken pieces of the vase, hidden between the linens in a trunk in Jean-Luc's room. With the pieces were flattened paper flowers. Painted purple. When I confronted Jean-Luc, he began to cry, telling me he had wanted to cheer me up, one day in March. It was the spring his father . . . left. It was a bad time for us. He had made the paper irises, and he had broken the vase getting it out of the cupboard. He was too frightened to confess.

"Jean-Luc rarely cried as a boy. His father punished him for it. But once he started that day, he was unable to stop. It was as if he was crying all the tears his father had not allowed. Crying for his father, for the loss he couldn't understand. I could not scold him, but comforted him, telling him it didn't matter, I wasn't mad at him. The next day he drew this picture for me." She slowly ran her hands over the paper on her lap.

"Later, as a young man, when he told me that he would not become a priest, and saw my anger, he painted the same picture for me. I know now it was his way of telling me something, of begging me to understand, as I had that day so long ago, but my disappointment was too deep. He was my only son. Every mother has dreams for her child."

She stopped for a minute, her eyes flickering to Sylvie's, then she continued. "I told him I didn't want his picture, didn't want any of them, didn't want to ever see them again. The next day they were gone."

Her twisted fingers reached for the little coloured card in Sylvie's hand. "When I saw this, after school today, I . . ." She set the card, gently, on top of the larger picture in her lap.

The women sat beside each other, looking down at the two pictures.

Madame Painchaud finally spoke. "This envelope is for you. For Raymond. They are all the pictures Jean-Luc drew as a child. And the pictures Raymond made, in school. At first, I couldn't put them up, could hardly look at them; they brought such an ache." She sighed, a long, heavy sigh. "I thought that you, and the boy, would like them. Raymond's pictures, and those of his father. I only wish to keep these." She touched the two on her lap.

"Thank you," Sylvie said. She stood up, wiping her eyes with the back of her hand, and walked through the arch into the kitchen. "I will bring some tea."

In the kitchen she turned on the stove again. She put the teapot and two thick brown mugs on a small wooden tray, then went back to the arched doorway.

"Do you take sugar . . . ?"

Madame Painchaud was not in the living room. The envelope and pictures sat on the coffee table.

Sylvie looked down the short hallway off the living room. She saw Madame Painchaud standing in the doorway of Raymond's room, her hands folded together, her head bowed over them.

Sylvie went back to the kitchen. She poured the boiling water over the tea leaves in the teapot, looked at the two mugs on the tray. She reached into the cabinet in front of her and, standing on her toes, took a cardboard box off the top shelf.

Opening it and parting the layers of tissue paper, she lifted out two thin china cups and saucers covered with pink rosebuds. Then she set the mugs aside, arranged the cups and saucers beside the teapot on the tray, and carried it into the living room.

THE ORANGE

I STAND IN FRONT OF THE DEEP stained sink, peeling
the orange and listening to the dull scrape of the knife
behind me. My mother sits on a bench at the scrubbed
wooden table, paring potatoes onto a piece of newspaper.

When all the thick orange rind is neatly stacked on the
counter beside the sink, I start at the pith, carefully pulling
off each webby white vein and putting it in a pile beside the
rind. I pick until there is nothing left to uncover. The
orange sits in my hand, a perfect naked ball.

Something happened today, I say, looking at it.

My mother makes a sound in her throat.

A man said something to me. In town, while I was
waiting for my ride home.

The knife is suddenly silent. I begin to separate the
sections of orange, laying each wedge on the counter in
front of the two piles. Then I hear the knife start to work
again, quick sharp scrapes.

The sections are in a straight line when she finally speaks.

What kinda thing he say?

Just something. Something . . . bad, I guess. Wanted me to do something bad.

I don't move. I feel her watching me.

Somethin' dirty, you mean?

I nod, tracing the silky surface of one section.

The knife slows, then scrapes harder and faster. Stops.

But he didn't do nuthin?

No.

I hear a sound, maybe the wind around the windows, maybe a sigh. The scraping starts again, each pull of the knife long and even.

No, I say again. Because of the rain. He said he'd wait for me another day, when it wasn't so wet. He gave me this orange. Pulled my hand out, put the orange in it, made me take it. Told me now I owed him.

The smooth orange segments have become a circle, joined end to end. An open flower.

Someone you seen before?

Maybe, I say, turning around. The glare of the bulb hanging from the ceiling is making deep black hollows under my mother's eyes. Might be one of the men working out at Jensen's, I tell her. He's got a lot, this harvest. Might be one of them.

Her eyes drop to the bowl of potatoes in front of her. Well, most likely he'll be gone soon then, she says, standing and folding the paper over the peelings with slow rustling whispers. Jensen's place be done by the weekend, she adds.

A burst of rain, loud as a handful of gravel, hits the window. She looks into the bare blackness of the glass, holding the newspaper against her chest. Then she puts the bundle onto the bench. No oranges in town this time a year, she says.

She walks to the sink and stands beside me. One thing's true, she tells the calendar over the sink. We've had a lot of rain this fall.

Still studying the picture of the grain elevator with the sun setting behind it, she gathers up the orange peel, the pile of pith, and the eleven sections, one for each of my years, and throws them into the slop pail under the sink.

She finally turns to face me. I look at her. Her mouth opens, closes. I watch the colourless lips open one more time.

Set the table, she says. It's almost supper time. They'll be in soon, lookin' for their meal.

She takes the potatoes from the table and dumps them into the water boiling in the battered aluminum pot. I throw the green oilcloth across the table, try to spread it so it lies flat. The fold lines rise back up.

Men's always sayin' things. Don't mean nuthin.

Her voice is hard to hear over the pounding of the rain and the bubble and spatter from the pot.

What? I say, even though I heard her. What?

She comes over and leans across the table. She starts smoothing out the oilcloth. As she bends her head, I see the white of her scalp, the skin shiny under the thin brown hair.

Don't mean nuthin, she repeats. Usually don't amount to nuthin, the things men go on about. But you keep yourself out the way when they start up, all the same.

I watch her red chapped knuckles, her long fingers spreading and smoothing the cloth over and over, even though there isn't a single wrinkle left.

You member that, girl, what I say about men. Most specially, you don't ever have to owe no man nuthin. You hear me, now? Say you hear me.

I keep watching her hands, brown and red, moving across the green cloth. They're pressing hard, but gentle, the same way I see her dry off the new calves each year.

I hear you, I say. I hear you.

ORDER IN THE HOUSE

IT WAS MY NEIGHBOUR and sometime friend, Marliss, who brought up what she called my obsessive behaviour. She pointed out that my frenzied housecleaning began precisely at the time I had eaten the final slice of banana loaf and thrown out the last browned chrysanthemum and daisy arrangement.

It was a relief to be rid of the reminders. The cake and the flowers had been two of the many offerings from the elderly women I met that day. I couldn't keep them straight; their names all seemed to start with a vowel—Alma, Eunice, Ida, Olive. The only thing I remember about them, those old friends of my mother, was that they had names and hats that were out of fashion.

"Don't you get it, Wanda?" Marliss said, watching me use a toothpick to clean around the aluminum edge of the sink where it met the counter. "It's an act, a symbolic act. Cleaning your house is like clearing away all the junk that went on between you and your mom." She opened a cupboard. "Now that she's gone, you're cleansing the negative feelings you harboured towards her. Where are all your ashtrays?"

"I only smoke on the back porch now," I said. "The whole place was starting to stink; it gets into everything, and I just had the carpet shampooed." I pushed Wiley aside with my knee. He groaned low in his throat and went to his bed beside the fridge, pushing at the neatly folded blanket with his nose until he had it worked into the right tangle.

"Geez, Wanda. I think you ought to see someone. Maybe there's a name for what you've got." Marliss put her unlit cigarette to her lips, took it out again. "How about post-matriarchal depression? Like post-partum. Get it? The new-baby blues, the dead-mother blues."

The toothpick snapped between my fingers. "I don't believe in symbolic acts. A deed is simply a deed. You're hungry, you eat." I started to unpack the bag of groceries sitting on the counter, stopped for a minute, a head of lettuce in one hand, to look at her. "You take a Continuing Ed course in Human Dynamics at the community club, Marliss, you turn into a junior shrink."

I put the lettuce in the fridge, went back to the bag. "The house is dirty, you clean it. That's it. It has nothing to do with my mother."

I opened my spice drawer and tried to wrestle a new bottle of celery seed in between the cardamon and the cloves. It wouldn't fit without me taking out the coriander at the end of the row and rearranging the whole drawer. I slammed the drawer shut and banged the bottle down on the counter.

Marliss shook her head. "Look at you, Wanda. Worrying about the alphabetical order of spices is something your mother would have done. What's up? I mean, you never even seemed to *like* her. You were always complaining about her, telling me how she bugged you, how she fussed over you. Remember the business with the breadbox?"

I looked at the square wooden box with its neat black lettering. The 'R' just under the little knob on the door was worn away, so the box said B EAD. I detested breadboxes.

They were a waste of counter space, a tiny dinosaur left over from my childhood. Every modern kitchen of the fifties sported a breadbox that matched the graduated canister set, with its large and important FLOUR container down to the squat, insignificant TEA.

My mother's kitchen had been modern. She had been a modern woman, the television mother of the fifties. Now everyone laughs at those old *Father Knows Best* and *Leave It to Beaver* mothers, but those women were my mother's idols. Every morning she wore a crisp housedress with a clean apron tied over it. Some of those aprons even had a frilly bib front.

And she longed for me to be the television daughter. To have a tidy bedroom and a ponytail and a glowing complexion. To wear a pink orlon sweater set, the cardigan held together with a fake pearl sweater clip, modestly covering my surprising new breasts from the eager eyes of newspaper boys and pimply cashiers at the Tom-Boy.

I disappointed her in all departments. Room, clothes, and looks. I set the precedent when I was a teenager, and I never stopped disappointing her.

My mother had brought the breadbox over one afternoon.

"I bought a new one last weekend, in Grand Forks. Did you know I went to Grand Forks, Wanda?"

I shook my head, sitting on the kitchen floor and carefully clipping Wiley's nails. As one of the nails flew against the front of the stove with a tiny click, I heard my mother's intake of breath.

"I went down with Marge Ogrodnick and her husband. Stan. Stan drives Marge down any time she hears about a big sale. You wouldn't believe how cheap she gets paper towels, Wanda."

"Mmm-hmm." I stroked Wiley's silky paw. "All done, big boy." He licked the back of my hand, slowly. I turned my hand over and let him lick my palm.

"I hope you'll wash before you do anything else, Wanda. Anyway, I got a new breadbox at the Target store. You know how I like their housewares section. And the first thing I thought, when I bought my new breadbox, was, well, now Wanda can have my old one."

She swept aside my Red Zinger teabags, threw out an untouched wheat-germ-and-sesame muffin, and piled a stack of stained coffee mugs in the sink. Before she set the breadbox down in the cleared space, she ran her fingertips over the counter, rubbed them together and shook her head. Then she scooped my loaf of Hovis from its usual place on top of the toaster, firmly setting it on the breadbox's one shelf.

"There," she said, surveying the lonely loaf. "That's much better. You've just got to get yourself organized, Wanda. You're asking for trouble, leaving food and dirty dishes out on the counter. You'll have your whole kitchen infested if you're not careful."

"Mother," I said, "I've yet to know anyone who's actually had an infestation in their kitchen."

"You know what I mean," she said. She opened my fridge, looked inside, closed it. "I don't see how you can live the way you do. But it's not my business. It's up to you, Wanda. You're the only one who can put your house in order. Some nights I just can't rest, worrying about you."

That had been about a month before she died. Her death was the only time in her life she wasn't prepared. It caught both of us off guard.

I stared at the breadbox, then looked around my unfamiliar, spotless kitchen. Marliss was still standing in front of me, eating a Fig Newton she'd found on her quest for an ashtray.

"Maybe you're right, Marliss. Maybe there's something I have to straighten out." I took the half-eaten cookie out of her hand and tossed it in Wiley's dog dish, walked across the gleaming linoleum and opened the back door.

Marliss looked at the door, down at Wiley, half-heartedly sniffing the Fig Newton, back to the door, and finally to my face.

"You're losing it, Wanda. I'm only trying to help."

"I know you are, Marliss. Thanks." My voice was even, noncommittal. "I just remembered something. Something I have to do."

After she'd left, I picked up the breadbox and carried it out through the porch, down the steps, all the way to the back lane. I stood there for a few minutes, just holding the wooden box, running my fingers over the smooth surface. I stopped at the missing R, touching the blank space and thinking of the countless times my mother's knuckles must have rubbed there, opening and closing the breadbox door.

I gently placed the box on top of the empty milk cartons and the crushed cereal box and the remains of yesterday's zucchini casserole. I looked at it for a moment, sitting so . . . primly, on top of the garbage, then took it out. Holding it against my chest, I went to the garage and found a cardboard box. Back in the house I opened the storage cupboard under the stairs, and wedged the box onto one of the crowded shelves, between the photo albums from my first marriage and a shopping bag of high-school track trophies.

I got my cigarettes from the porch, then sat down at the kitchen table and lit one, dragging deeply and blowing the smoke towards the crisply ironed gingham curtains beside me. I realized I hadn't brought an ashtray in from the porch, started to get up, then sat back down, pulling the trailing lemon geranium on the window ledge closer.

I watched the long, trembling ash, thinking about the cardboard box in the cupboard.

Wiley raised his head from his paws, his tail thumping once on the floor, as if I'd whispered his name.

I smiled at him, then tapped the ash into the geranium's spongy soil.

QUESTIONS TO ASK A TURTLE

THE GIRLS ARE EATING Froot Loops at the kitchen table when she comes downstairs. Val doesn't usually buy Froot Loops, but when they'd been grocery shopping this week and both Tina and Rachel had started fussing about them, pestering her to buy them, she didn't have the energy to put up a fight.

Tina is reading out loud, some sort of comic digest propped up against the cereal box. Her bowl is full to the top, the little hollow circles swimming in milk tinted a peachy colour. Rachel has no milk in her bowl, and arranges the pink and orange and yellow loops into three separate piles.

They both look up as Val crosses to the counter and starts to fill the coffee pot with water. She feels them watching as she puts a filter into the coffeemaker and spoons in the ground coffee. As she turns the button to ON, she looks at them. Rachel quickly lowers her head, goes back to her sorting. Tina's eyes return to the page in front of her, then she taps it with the tip of her spoon.

"Listen to this, Mom. Listen." She glances back up, to make sure Val is looking at her. "It's really funny."

"O.K." Val bunches her hair at the nape of her neck, takes an elastic out of the pocket of her shorts, and winds it around the hair. She sits down beside Tina.

"Princess Te Kawa . . . kaw, something, an Orpington chicken from New Zealand, laid 361 eggs in 364 days. Her egg record is still unbroken."

Val turns her head slightly and looks out the window over Tina's head. Tina can read anything, even though she's only eight.

Rachel is more like me, Val thinks. I hope she doesn't have trouble in school. She studies the tops of the trees again. They're motionless. Even after the cool breeze last night, it looks like it will be another hot day.

There's a tapping on her forearm. Tina, and her spoon. "Did you hear that, Mom? About the eggs? But listen, this is even weirder." She tucks her hair behind her ears.

" 'Helmut Wurlinger of Austria loved to walk, but not on his feet. To get from Vienna to Munich in 1910, he started walking on his hands—and made it!' That's far, isn't it? From Vienna to Munich? How far is it? Farther than from our house to Grandma's?"

"Farther than where Daddy is?" Rachel asks, holding a pink Froot Loop up to her eye. She looks at Val through the hole.

Val wonders, for a second, what will happen if just this once, she doesn't answer. But Tina is looking at her, waiting. So is Rachel.

"Way farther than Grandma's," Val says. She thinks about her mother, what her mother said to her yesterday. She takes one of the dry little circles out of Rachel's bowl, rolls it between her fingers.

She hadn't wanted to tell her mother, tell her what she'd found out last week. What Eric had done. She was filled with shame at having to say the words. But she could never keep anything from her mother, from Shirl, with her fruity

140

little eyes and pursed mouth. Shirl always found out everything.

"I knew it. Knew something was up. So, who was it? One of your girlfriends?" Shirl asked, sitting at Val's kitchen table.

Val felt her mouth stitching into a knot that matched Shirl's. "I don't know her; she's from over near Morris."

Shirl lit a cigarette. "You got proof?" she asked, holding the cigarette high, up beside her ear, her elbow resting on the table.

"I wish you wouldn't smoke in here, Mom," Val said, sprinkling Ajax on a striped dishcloth and starting to scrub at the aluminum sink.

Shirl ignored her, taking a deep pull. "You got proof?" she repeated. "You know for sure?"

Val scrubbed harder.

"Well, he'll be back. They always come back, after they've had their fun."

"It's not like that, Mom. He says it's over; he hasn't seen her for a long time."

"And you believe him?"

Val stopped wiping. She put the dishrag down and leaned against the counter, crossing her arms over her chest. "Yes. I believe him, that it's over. But that doesn't mean it's the end of it. Not for me."

Shirl blew smoke out in a long, ruffled cloud. "Your father was the same. Nothing you can do about it; take it from me. Best to try and forget it, act like nothing happened, when he comes back. They're always sorry once they leave, realize what they had. Always come back."

Val looked down, watched her bare toe trace a square of linoleum. "He didn't leave. I told him to get out. Told him he couldn't come back."

She looked up when she heard the annoyed smack of her mother's lips.

"Well, that was pretty dumb," Shirl said. "You'd better untell him. Make up with him, get him back where he belongs, looking after you and the kids. You call him back now, Val."

Val looked sideways at her mother. "No. I don't want him. Not after this. Maybe you could do it, Mom, take Dad back, but I can't. I just can't."

Shirl stubbed out her cigarette, grinding it hard into the ashtray. "Now look, Val. You don't find a man like Eric every day. One with a steady job, don't drink too much, gets you and the kids what you need. Treats you pretty darn good, if you ask me. So you be glad for what you got, and you learn to bite your tongue. Take it from me, Val, you'll be sorry if you kick him out for good."

Val turned her back to her mother, picking up the rag again. She held it in her hands, studying the blue and green stripes.

"But I can't love him, Mom, not the way I used to. Not when I think about him with someone else."

Shirl got up and walked over to the counter. She stood beside Val, close, but not touching her. "Look, Val." Her voice was softer than usual. "I know it's hard, but that's just the way it is. You kick him out, next thing you know you can't pay the rent on this place, and then where'll you be? What are you gonna do? Your job don't pay that much, and the girls . . . think about the girls, Val. They're gonna be wanting lotsa stuff, stuff you won't be able to afford. And then you start going to pieces. Remember what a mess I got myself into, when I let it get to me that one time? What a mess it was for you kids, too?"

Val closed her eyes.

"Love, schmuv, is what I say," Shirl said, putting out one hand and patting Val, gingerly, on the bare shoulder. "You want love, go to a movie. Read one of them pocket books. You can't expect the love you're talking about after . . . how many years since yous tied the knot? Eight, nine?"

"Nine." Val's eyes were still closed.

"Well, there you go. What you look for in a marriage is what you got right here. A decent house, a coupla kids, and a man. You're a family, Val, you and Eric and the kids. And families gotta stick together." She stopped to pick a tiny fleck of tobacco off her tongue. "You got it all, Val. So don't go lousing it up. Find out where Eric is and tell him to get back here. That's the only answer to all this."

Val leaned over the edge of the sink, rested her arms on it and put her forehead on her bent arms.

Shirl looked at her. She put her thick hand on Val's back and rubbed it in one big, slow circle. "I know, baby." Her hand stopped at the bottom of the circle. "But just think about what it was like when your dad took off, those times. Think about it. You want that for your kids? Do you?"

Val puts the yellow Froot Loop in her mouth. "Lemony," she says, and smiles.

There is a tiny breath of air, a whisper, from the open window over the table. The drooping heads of the African violets on the window sill tremble. Then Rachel looks at Tina, and they both turn to Val, and smile back. Their smiles are big, and tight.

Later, standing at the sink, washing the breakfast dishes, Val looks out the window in front of her, at the weedy grass of the backyard, at the rusting swing set, at the vegetable garden, growing tired and untidy this last week. At one end of the garden is a decrepit potting shed with a slanted roof of rotting green plastic, at the other end a stretch of chicken wire nailed between two posts. The chicken wire sags beneath the weight of the sweet peas that wind up and around it.

Beyond the yard trails a dusty back lane that is hardly used anymore, not since the new front road was put in, over three years ago.

The girls are out there, now, on the old lane. Standing

with her hands in the warm, soapy water, Val can see them bending over, Rachel's short curly dark hair, like hers, Tina's long and straight and fair.

As she watches, Tina turns and starts running, across the yard toward the house.

"Come see, come see what we found," Tina yells. "You have to come right now, Mom! It's out in the ditch!" As Val walks across the kitchen, Tina bursts in through the screen door and grabs Val's hand. "Quick, before he gets away."

"What is it?" Val brushes a stray piece of hair away from her eyes. Her forehead feels damp, the skin tender, as if all the tiny blood vessels under the bone of her skull are waiting to erupt into a headache. The wooden back steps are dry and hot, creaking under her bare feet.

"It's a turtle, a huge turtle. Is it still there, Rachel?" Tina calls, pulling hard on Val's hand as she leads her down the steps and onto the long, scratchy grass.

Val can see Rachel's small figure crouching on her heels in the dust, her back to them. She jumps up and turns, cupping her hands around her mouth.

"Yeah! Just sitting. It's not moving. Hurry up!" She waves both her arms at them, performing a jigging dance, plumes of tan dust curling up around her ankles and calves.

I should cut some of the sweet peas, Val thinks, noticing the thickness of the blossoms as they pass the flowered screen. Maybe I'll cut two, one for the kitchen table, one for the coffee table. It would look pretty.

She remembers the way Eric always commented on the flowers she put around the house. He noticed things like that, liked little changes. Flowers, or if she tried putting stewed tomatoes instead of tomato sauce in the lasagna. If she wore a different perfume.

No. I won't bother, Val tells herself. I may as well look at them from the kitchen window.

"There it is," Tina says, her voice dropping to a reverent whisper. "Look. Right there."

Val bends forward and looks into the buzzing heat of the weedy gully. A large turtle, one side of its shell split, sits unblinking.

"Where do you—" Rachel starts, but with a hissing "Shhh!" from Tina, starts again, voice barely a whisper. "Where do you think it came from, Mom? And what happened to the shell? Does it hurt?" She takes a step closer to the turtle, squats and reaches out a finger.

"We don't have to whisper," Val says, "but don't touch him. Or her. I don't think that kind of turtle bites, but it might be scared and snap at you."

Rachel immediately pulls her finger away, stands and backs up against Val.

"I really don't know where it came from," Val says. "Pelican Lake is ten miles from here."

"There was a turtle that once walked 1500 miles," Tina says, "across two states. I read it in my FACTS-ination book. Someone painted the date and place on its shell, and it was found two states away. But what about that big crack, on the side there, Mom? What do you think happened?"

"Maybe it got hit by a car," Rachel says.

"You're probably right." Val looks at the greeny-brown shell. The split is a wide inverted V at the edge, then narrows in until it's a fine seam. The open edges of the crack are a darker green than the rest of the shell. She picks up a twig, holds it in front of the turtle's face. It blinks, turns its head slightly to one side. "I bet it was walking on the lane here, maybe at night, and a truck hit it. It might have gone flying and cracked its shell on a rock, or maybe it was just the impact of the tire."

"What's a impat?" Rachel pulls a foxtail out of the pebbly shoulder of the ditch and inches closer to the turtle.

"Impact. Just the force of the tire." Val watches Rachel. "One quick blow, hitting it and breaking it open."

Rachel gives the turtle's head a swipe with the foxtail. It slowly pulls its head toward its shell.

"Don't tease it," Val says.

"Do you think it hurts? Can something hard, like a shell, hurt?" Tina says, pulling a long piece of hair over her eyes. She doesn't wait for an answer. "And can we keep it, Mom? Can we? For a pet?" Tina says, still keeping her eyes covered with her hair. "You said we could get a pet when we were old enough. You said."

"You said, you said," Rachel echoes.

"I said maybe. But we couldn't keep this big old thing, sweetie. It's wild. It wouldn't be happy. And you couldn't really play with it or anything."

Tina drops her hair and bends over the turtle. "Could we keep it for just today? Or maybe just until Dad comes back?"

Val looks at the girl's long thin neck, the hair hanging on either side of it. She looks at the tiny knobby bones above the top of her T-shirt.

"Well, we shouldn't leave it here. It might get hit again, or a dog will bother it. We'll keep it until tomorrow, and then we'll take it over to Pelican Lake, and put it back in the water, O.K.? And maybe we can drive around to the beach side, go for a swim while we're there. One last swim."

Now Tina stands and faces her. "One last swim before what?" Her voice seems grown-up, hard. It surprises Val.

She tosses the twig into the ditch. "Before summer's over."

"There's still a whole week before school starts. It's not over yet."

"Yeah! Let's go swimming," Rachel says. "Maybe Daddy will come back today, and he could come with us. Will he be back today, Mom? From his business? I could stand on his shoulders, and he can throw me in, like he did last time. You too, Tina, he could throw you, too."

Tina bends over the turtle again.

"He could throw us, couldn't he, Mommy? He could throw us, like before," Rachel says.

Val runs her hand over Rachel's hair. "I'll get the big washtub. We'll load it in there, and then you girls go get your wagon, and we'll pull it up to the house."

Tina straightens up.

"We can make it lunch," Rachel says. "What do turtles eat, Tina?"

Tina turns her back to Val. "Well, I think they like grass, and probably celery. Maybe apples. Crunchy stuff. I think I'm gonna name him . . . let's see." The little-girl's voice Val knows has returned, and as she starts back toward the house their voices float behind her.

"No, Tina, I wanna think of a name. You always name everything."

"Well, you think of the first name, and I'll think of the middle one."

"Kermit. I'm gonna name him Kermit."

"NO. That's stupid, Rach. That's a frog's name, not a—"

The voices are cut off as Val opens the door to the little shed, crowded with an old push lawnmower, two rakes— one metal and one bamboo—a coil of faded hose, and a sagging cardboard box of gardening paraphernalia, trowels and gloves and clippers and a pair of rusty shears. Val steps inside and her eyes search in the dimness, along the wall. She spots the old washtub, and above it, hanging on a nail, she sees Eric's coveralls, the grey ones with the zipper permanently stuck halfway down, the coveralls he uses for working on his truck, for dirty jobs around the house. At the sight of them, hanging empty and still, she shuts the door behind her. It's suffocatingly hot, muggy, in the tiny shed. The sun splinters emerald through the cracked plastic roof; Val feels a watery, floating sensation in her thighs and stomach. She leans her back against the door and stands there for a minute, letting the crushing green heat envelop her, looking at the outline of the coveralls. She slides down the door, sitting on the hard dirt floor, staring at the coveralls until she finds it hard to breathe. Then she hoists herself up and goes over to them. Running her hands slowly over the fabric, soft and smooth with age, she suddenly gathers it in both hands and presses her face into it, taking deep breaths.

After a while, she turns and takes the shears out of the cardboard box. Feeling one slow trickle of sweat running down between her breasts, she opens the blades and places them, carefully and slowly, on one of the sleeves of the coveralls. She closes the blades. She opens and closes them again, and again. The blades are dull; the grey fabric just folds over them. She opens and closes the shears harder, faster, until she's making tiny grunts with the effort and frustration, but the coveralls just hang there, uncut, swaying on their nail.

Finally Val stops. She wipes her forehead with the back of her arm, puts the shears back into the box and runs her hands over her cheeks, across her eyes. Then she picks up the washtub and steps out. The air outside now seems light, almost fragrant, and the whiteness of the August morning is nearly blinding.

That evening, after the girls are in bed, Val goes to the back door to switch the porch light off. She looks out at the washtub, then opens the screen door.

She stands there, holding the door and looking down at the turtle. It's still moving, the way it started a few minutes after they set it in the tub, on a bed of grass pulled out of the lawn. It's moving with the same restless, pointless activity, squarish front feet ponderously trying to climb up the smooth sides of the tub, thick toenails clicking. Its feet get six inches from the bottom of the tub, then slide down again. Val keeps watching.

And even after she gets into bed, upstairs, far from the back porch and the washtub, she can't get to sleep, imagining she still hears that endless, futile beat.

Val has just started to make the sandwiches when she hears Eric's truck pull in beside the house. Without looking up, she finishes peeling the banana. She starts to cut it, but something's wrong with the knife; some of the sticky round slices are thick and uneven, some chopped in half. She doesn't turn as Eric comes through the kitchen, but the corner of her mouth starts a tiny, frenzied dance. She digs the knife into the jar of peanut butter.

"Hello," Eric says, walking behind Val. Stopping.

Val stops, too, stops her brisk spreading of peanut butter. There is a large tear in the centre of the soft bread.

"Daddy! Daddy!" Rachel rushes into the kitchen. "Daddy. I knew you'd come. We're going swimming. Come on, Dad, get your bathing suit, you can come, too. Don't you want to come?"

Val's hands stay still, the only visible movement at the side of her mouth. She starts on the sandwiches again after she feels Eric move away from her.

"It's a good day for swimming," he says to Rachel, picking her up with one arm, "and it's going to get even . . ." He stops. "Hi, Tina, hi honey." His voice is quieter. "How are you?"

Val looks over to see Tina standing in the doorway.

"I'm O.K., Dad. Where's your suitcase?"

Eric doesn't hesitate. "I left it in the truck. I was so anxious to see you, I didn't want to wait to bring it in. Come here, give me a big hug."

Val hears the padding of Tina's bare feet, the rustle of clothes. Tina's voice is muffled. "I missed you, Daddy. You were gone so long."

"I know, Tina."

"Get your bathing suit, Daddy," Rachel says. "Get it right now. We're going as soon as Mommy finishes, oh, and Daddy!" She's panting. "We found a *huge* turtle. Did you see him, in the washtub on the porch?"

"No."

"We found him yesterday, and we're going to take him to Pelican Lake, when we go swimming. Now you can carry the washtub. It's too heavy for Mommy. Isn't it, Mommy? Too heavy. Daddy can carry it, right?"

"Maybe Daddy's too tired to come with us. After his long trip." Val keeps her voice neutral.

Rachel giggles. "Daddy never gets tired, do you, Daddy? You're not tired, right?"

As Val waits to hear the answer, slowly placing each banana slice on top of the peanut butter, Eric swoops Rachel up in the air. Val listens to Rachel's delighted whooping as Eric throws her again and again. She glances toward the kitchen table where Tina is sitting now, watching Rachel and Eric, her fingers playing with one page of the book in front of her, folding and unfolding the corner.

Val keeps making sandwiches and carefully cutting them into identical, neat triangles, until there are too many for them to possibly eat.

Val stops the car a quarter of a mile before the public beach, parking it along the side of the road. They all get out, and Eric flips open the back door of the station wagon. He lifts the washtub out with one swift heave, and Val sees the swell of his biceps. She looks away.

"There's a bit of a path this way," she says to the girls. "We used to . . . you can fish down here."

"Did you catch lots of fish?"

"Sometimes, Rachel," Eric says. "Lead the way, Val."

The four of them start down the rough, narrow trail, Val first, holding Rachel's hand, then Tina, then Eric and the washtub.

"Is it heavy, Dad?" Tina asks.

"Not too bad," Eric says. "But I wouldn't want to have to go too far with this old guy. Whatcha got in your knapsack, Tina Turnip?"

"Dad! I don't like that name. And it's some paint."

"Paint?" The word comes out in a whoosh of air. "What's the paint for?"

"We're going to paint on the turtle's shell, before we set him loose."

Eric's breathing is getting ragged. The path is steeper, narrower, and Val goes slower, her sneakers sliding on the loose earth. She turns around, looking at Eric and her children. Their faces are covered in dappled shadows.

"Almost there," she says, pushing the feathery branch of a poplar out of the way. Then, "You alright back there?"

"Yup. Don't stop," Eric says.

They step out of the wooded area, onto a low plateau of smooth rocks and gravelly sand. Eric sets the tub down with a soft thud.

Tina shrugs off her backpack and unzips it. She takes out a small jar of paint and a paintbrush, and takes the lid off the jar.

"What are you planning to paint, Tina?" Eric asks, looking at the shiny black liquid.

Rachel winds her hands around his arm. "We're gonna paint our names. Tina read it in a book, how people did that."

"Then if someone else ever finds it, they'll know where it's from," Tina explains. She flips one long pale braid over her shoulder, turns to Eric. "But this paint won't hurt the turtle, Dad. Mom phoned and found out. And it won't wash off in the water, either. It'll stay forever."

She dips the brush into the paint, and then stoops over the tub. She dips and paints, dips and paints, and finally stands back.

"There. Pelican Lake, Manitoba. Tina. Here, Rachel, you can put your name, too." She hands the brush to Rachel. "But don't make your name really big. You always print so big."

"No I don't," Rachel says, and they all wait while she fashions each letter of her name on the hard shell, under Tina's small neat printing. Her bottom lip is sucked in with the effort. "Now you, Mom."

Val takes the brush from Rachel.

"Put Val and Eric," Tina says, a little too loudly. Val recognizes the demanding, adult tone from yesterday. "Val and Eric. Write it, Mom."

151

Val doesn't look up. She quickly prints the two names, then screws the lid back on the jar. Tina stares down into the tub.

"Good," she breathes, "O.K." She steps back. "Dad, get him out."

They stand behind Eric as he lifts the turtle out and sets it down on the rocky shore. It lifts its head, eyes blinking. It stays there for a minute, as if sniffing the air, then starts towards the water, putting each foot forward slowly, tentatively, as if testing the ground.

"It's going, it's going," Rachel squeals. "It's gonna go in the water."

"Go, Kermit, go," Tina says, taking a step behind it. "Go home and find your family."

Val smiles, for the first time that day. "We should have set him down closer to the edge. We'll be standing here for ages at this rate."

"We're not in any hurry, are we?" Eric says, taking a sideways step towards her, his eyes never leaving the turtle. His arm is nearly against hers.

Tina picks up a flat rock, throws it into the water. "This place is neat," she says, looking around. "It would be a neat place to go camping."

"Yeah! Let's go camping, let's go camping," Rachel yells.

"Summer's nearly over," Val says. All of a sudden she feels Eric's hand on her shoulder. It rests lightly.

"But we could come here next year, couldn't we Dad?" Tina says. "We could all come camping here next summer."

There are a few seconds of silence.

"That's up to your mom," Eric says. His hand feels heavier now, warmer. "What do you think, Val? Do you think we can go camping next summer?" They're both watching the turtle's progress.

The question seems to resonate in the motionless air. Val feels the words pulsing around her face, feels them settle on her shoulders, their warm burden confused with the weight of Eric's hand.

She sees that the turtle has made it to the edge of the water. Its neck is stretched forward, and the slow lumbering seems to have increased by a fraction of a second.

"Maybe," Val says, the word coming from nowhere, surprising her. She watches as the turtle's front foot touches the water. "Maybe we'll go camping."

The turtle's feet begin to move in an eager rhythm, and suddenly, in one swift and unexpected graceful movement, it disappears into a bed of dark weeds that sprout from the shallow water.

Val studies the spot where the turtle has submerged. She wonders about the crack in its shell, and whether the cool water will feel comforting, a soothing balm, or whether it will bite and sting, like vinegar.

SIGHS FOR LILA

WHENEVER LILA PHONED her father, Vittorio, from Toronto, he told her about his week, what he had eaten, who he had seen, what the doctor had said. As his voice grew slower, fainter, Lila began to imagine a heaviness resting in the second of silence between questions and answers, something unsaid. It quivered, waiting.

Finally Lila came home.

But back on her old street, she still couldn't escape the sombre women in black, the unadorned, the pious, the females of her father's generation. Lila rarely saw one alone; they were always in groups, like a flock of grackles in the fall, moving busily together, shoulders touching, beaked faces pecking, prodding. When Lila passed them, clustered around the olive barrels in Marinelli Brothers, or on the steps outside Holy Rosary after Sunday morning mass, she felt their stares.

She knew what they thought of her for what had happened so long ago. But this time she wouldn't leave, not until she told her father, said what she had wanted to say, needed to say, all these years.

After a week of spending each day in the hospital beside her father's bed, Lila was tired of the rotating menu of cafeteria food.

She rooted through the freezer of the fridge in the kitchen of her old home, finding two trays of cloudy, metallic-smelling ice cubes, a bag of dinner rolls, a pint of congealed strawberry ice cream, and one plastic container with "Spezzato" written across the top in her father's shaky scrawl. She set the container of homemade stew on a paper towel on the Formica counter, to thaw for tomorrow, and then looked under the sink. Her father's dented, wide-mouthed metal thermos was still there, even though he hadn't worked in the last eleven or twelve years. Lila traced the impressions on the sides of the thermos, thinking of her father's work-thickened fingers and the roundness of his chest, the ruddy colour of his cheeks, the shiny waves in his black hair. The way he used to be, the way Lila liked to think of him.

He had worked at two jobs for all of Lila's childhood. Lila never knew why; whether it was because they needed the money or because he just liked to work. His day job was with Perillo Masonry, repairing chimneys and laying walkways, or creating fronts and courtyards for restaurants, complete with arches and fountains and coloured tiles set in between the bricks.

In the evening he worked as a watchman at a downtown office building. He wore a clean shirt and pressed trousers, and, carrying a jingling set of keys, walked up and down the halls, checking doors and occasionally shining his flashlight into a dark corner.

When he came home from working all day with tile and bricks, he would be covered with the grey film of powdered mortar. Lila's mother would wait at the back door with an empty laundry basket and an old sheet. As soon as Vittorio stepped in and closed the door, her mother would hold the sheet up, and behind its protection Vittorio would take off his clothes and throw them in the basket. Then he would wrap the sheet around himself and walk across the gleaming kitchen linoleum, through the spotless living room to the bathroom. After twenty minutes Vittorio would emerge, freshly shaven, neatly dressed. They would all sit down for supper together before he left to catch the six o'clock downtown bus.

At eight or nine years old, Lila knew, without being told, or at least she didn't remember being told, that she was not to watch her father's back-door ritual. Still, she often tried to position herself, perhaps at the kitchen table, perhaps in her bedroom off the kitchen, so that she could peek over the top of a book or through the crack between the door and the frame, and see her father undress. She didn't know why she wanted to watch; she had heard, from some of the girls at school, that a naked man was something awful or funny, or both. Depending on which girl was reporting on seeing her father, brother, uncle, mother's boyfriend, the story would be told with mock horror and retching noises, or with smirks and giggles.

Lila always just listened; she had nothing to add, nothing to make the other girls shiver with disgust or delight. Lila knew her life was different from the lives of girls she went to school with. They had big, noisy families, with at least three or four sisters and brothers, sometimes many more. Nobody had a separate room, or even a bed to themselves.

Lila envied her classmates, these girls with saggy brown stockings and dresses that were too tight or too long, their lips and hands chapped in the winter, their knees skinned in the summer.

Her life was so ordered, so calm. Nothing ever changed, nothing happened, until her mother was killed, crossing a slippery winter street a month after Lila's twelfth birthday.

When they came home from the hospital the evening of the accident, Vittorio clutched a paper bag containing Lila's mother's shoes and purse and wedding ring. There was no clothing in the bag; Lila realized that the clothes must have been ruined. Perhaps the force the car struck with had torn the simple grey wool coat with the black mouton collar and the printed cotton dress underneath. Or perhaps the clothes had been cut to shreds. Lila knew the doctors and nurses sometimes used scissors to cut off people's clothes. If they needed to get at the body quickly, they didn't have time to undo rows of buttons, to unhook eyes, to unsnap stockings from garters and unlace and unzip and untie.

Betty Ann Wiltzer, who had been Lila's best friend in grade five, had once told her about the scissors. Betty Ann carried the faint muskiness of urine from sharing a bed with a little brother and sister, and had many stories to tell.

Lila tried not to imagine the sharp scissors slicing through her mother's dress, then through the full-body corset, the doughy flesh bursting free in front of complete strangers.

Lila's father quit his evening job, but all he did in the evenings was sit in one of the stiff chairs in the darkened living room, sometimes looking out the window, sometimes just staring straight ahead, into the kitchen. He seemed to be studying the stove. It made Lila nervous, seeing her father sitting and staring like that. At first she tried to talk to him, show him her school work. Vittorio would look at whatever Lila held in front of him, smile, and nod, then his eyes would waver, and his head would tilt, ever so slightly, to look around Lila, and she would see that he was staring at the stove again.

After a while she just stayed in her room once she had washed the supper dishes, sitting on her bed and doing her

homework or cutting out magazine pictures of animals for
her scrapbook or reading the latest Nancy Drew mystery.

Six months after her mother's accident, Lila started junior
high. She had no real friends in the noisy school with the
battered lockers and dingy narrow halls. She knew she had
nothing to attract the other girls—no older sister with a
wardrobe and diary to plunder, no older brother who might
attract a friend or two, no TV, no record player and pile of
45s to dance to, nothing. She hadn't had a best friend since
Betty Ann.

Lila was overcome with a desire to be more acceptable,
to be like the girls she admired, the girls with high
backcombed hair, thick pancake make-up, and puzzling
trails of small bruises on their heavily perfumed necks. Betty
Ann was now one of these girls, a girl with sideways glances
from under half-lowered lids, a swaying walk. She hadn't
bothered with Lila all through grade six, and while she
didn't exactly ignore Lila now, still saying "Hi, how's it
goin'?" when they passed in the hall, Lila felt the loss in her
life. She had loved being friends with Betty Ann, had loved
hearing all the stories Betty Ann had to tell, even though
she didn't understand most of them.

Sometimes, when Lila sat alone in her bedroom after
supper, she thought about Betty Ann, wondered what Betty
Ann was doing, who she was with. What she could do to
make Betty Ann be her friend again.

One lunch hour at the end of November Lila was in the
washroom. Just as she came out of the stall and started to
wash her hands, Betty Ann and Vera Lublenko came in. Lila
slowly dried her hands with a scratchy brown square of
paper and watched Betty Ann and Vera. They were taking
turns putting more coats of mascara on their already spiky,
separated lashes.

"So he says to me," Vera said, mouth open and one eye
closed as she leaned towards the wavy mirror over the sinks,

touching the end of the mascara brush to a quivering, spidery lash, "he says, you know how to spell my name? Of course I do, I goes, like I wouldn't know how to spell Harv. O.K., he says, then spell it. So I goes H A R V and he says nope, you got one letter wrong."

She handed the brush to Betty Ann, who spit into her palm and then touched the brush to it. She rubbed the brush into the square cake of mascara, then started in on her bottom lashes.

"What letter did you get wrong?" she asked, looking at Vera's reflection in the glass as she worked.

"That's what I asks. He says, and this is in the back row of Mr. Meckling's science class, Betty Ann, with Meckling right up there at his desk, he says, it's not a V, it's a D, and add the ON." She tries to control her giggling, waiting for Betty Ann to figure this out, and after a considerable length of time is rewarded by first a whoop and then a loud bray. The two girls laugh and choke and sputter, leaning against each other, watching themselves in the mirror.

"But that's not all," Vera continued, shaking Betty Ann's arm so hard the brush dropped into the sink. "When he says it he grabs my hand and tries to put it right *there!*"

Betty Ann doubled over, holding her abdomen, a few tiny squeaks forcing themselves out from between her shiny white lips. "Stop it, Vera, stop. My mascara's gonna be all over my face."

"Me too," Vera said. She yanked a paper towel from the dispenser and hunched over the sink, holding the square under her eyes and batting her lashes rapidly.

Lila watched the girls, a smile curling her lips up at each corner, so her mouth looked like a tight U.

Slowly, Betty Ann and Vera straightened up. They glanced over at Lila, nudged each other.

"Pretty funny, eh Lila?" Betty Ann said.

Lila nodded, the U still in place. "Yeah," she said.

"You get it, don't you, Lila?" Vera asked, her eyes sliding toward Betty Ann. Betty Ann coughed once.

"Sure I get it," Lila said. Her mind dashed from corner to corner, looking for a scrap, something to say, to keep her in the conversation. Something to show that she was one of them, that she understood their jokes, their laughter about boys. Then she said the only thing she knew that was remotely connected to the mysteries of the male body.

"My dad gets undressed under a sheet."

Vera and Betty Ann looked at each other. "Wow," Vera said. "Your dad gets undressed under a sheet." She sniggered.

Betty Ann took a step towards Lila. "So. He gets undressed under a sheet. Is he, like, shy, or what?"

Lila licked her lips. Betty Ann was talking to her, asking her a question. She couldn't let this moment pass.

"I don't know if he's shy. He just makes me hold the sheet for him while he undresses." This was a lie. Since Lila's mother died Vittorio had simply removed his caked boots after work, then walked through the house to the bathroom, his heavy steps leaving a trail of fine powder and tiny rocky particles.

"You hold a sheet, and he takes his clothes off?" Betty Ann said, glancing at Vera. "You mean like in bed? The sheet?"

"Yeah, a bedsheet." Lila felt braver, her voice got louder and she twirled a piece of her hair around one finger. "My mom used to do it, but . . . ," she shrugged, "now I have to. Every day when he gets home from work." She saw them looking at her, tried to drag it out. "But he doesn't take all his clothes off at once, just piece by piece."

"And then what?" Vera came up behind Betty Ann, looked over the girl's shoulder at Lila.

Lila was encouraged by the sudden interest in her. She laughed, and the loudness of her own laughter surprised her.

"Yeah, then what, Lila?" Betty Ann said. "What happens after your old man gets his clothes off?"

Lila couldn't say he went and took a shower. It would spoil the story. But she didn't know what Vera and Betty

161

Ann wanted to hear, so she took a chance. She shrugged again, smiled and said, "You know."

There was sudden silence in the washroom. Outside the wooden door feet pounded by, a locker slammed with a dull clang, and somewhere, far in the distance, a shrill scream sounded.

Finally, Betty Ann said, "You're kiddin'. You and the old guy?"

Lila just kept smiling, although something uncomfortable was tugging at her. She thought maybe it was because she wasn't really telling the truth about the sheet, but deep inside, she knew it was more than that, although she couldn't put her finger on it.

All afternoon Lila remembered the look on Betty Ann's face in the washroom, envisioning Betty Ann sitting down at her table in the lunchroom the next day, or maybe even inviting her over after school one day.

While she and her father were eating supper there was a knock on the front door. Vittorio got up to answer it. Lila heard voices, then her father came back to the kitchen. There were two policemen in blue uniforms behind him. One was carrying a brown envelope.

Lila put her fork neatly beside her plate.

"Lila," her father said. Lila stood up.

One policeman, the younger one, looked down at the two half-eaten plates of fried polenta and diced tomatoes, at the smaller side plates of salad, the jar of green olive oil. Then he looked at Lila. "We'd like to talk to you, miss." He glanced around the tidy kitchen. "Is there somewhere we could go, somewhere private?"

Lila turned to her father, but he was staring into the face of the young policeman.

"What's happened, Lila?" her father said, in Italian, still looking at the policeman. "Did something happen?"

The older policeman prodded Vittorio's arm, almost a

jab. "We'd rather speak to the young lady privately, Mr. Aiello," he said. His words are polite, but his voice was somehow unfriendly.

Lila had the same sick feeling as the day she saw her father standing outside the school fence, waiting for her. The day her mother died.

The young policeman looked behind Lila, to the bedroom with the pink chenille bedspread and the ballerina wallpaper. "Is that your room, Lila?" he asked.

Lila nodded.

"We'll go in there, for just a minute. To talk." He put his hand on her arm and steered her through the door, shutting it behind him. Lila sat down on the edge of her bed, her hands folded in her lap. She realized she was shivering.

"We got a call from the guidance counsellor at your school today, Lila," he said. "Mrs. Roth."

Lila nodded. She had never spoken to Mrs. Roth, but had seen her, in a small room beside the principal's office, and at assemblies. Mrs. Roth was never smiling.

"This afternoon, a teacher took a note from a student who was passing it to another girl. Because of the nature of the note, the teacher gave it to Mrs. Roth, and Mrs. Roth called the girl in to the office. The girl gave her some . . . details, and Mrs. Roth felt that it might be something we should check into." He looked down at Lila, at her teeth, slightly chattering. His voice softened. "There's nothing to be afraid of, Lila. Just tell the truth."

"About what?" Lila whispered.

The policeman cleared his throat, looked away, then opened the envelope and handed a crumpled lined sheet to Lila. The note had two misspelled sentences, written in letters familiar to Lila. Large, backhand letters, each small i topped with a little circle. "Lila Iallo's old man is doing it to her. Every night."

Lila kept her eyes fixed on the paper. She was ashamed to admit she didn't know what it meant. Without looking up, she passed the note back, then began to push each cuticle away from her nail, exposing tiny white moons.

"This is a serious implication, Lila. If you're in some kind of trouble, we want to know. We want to help you."

Lila didn't know if she was in trouble. She didn't know what implication meant, what the policeman wanted to hear. She sat there, pushing on her cuticles, until the man went out, softly clicking the door.

Again Lila heard the murmur of voices, then silence, then suddenly her father's voice, shouting. "No! What you saying? What, what! What is it? I no understand." Lila was ashamed of her father's heavily accented voice. She jumped as her door was flung open. Her father stood in the doorway, his cheeks a shocking crimson, his eyes huge and black. His lips were flapping against one another. The only time Lila had seen his lips shaking was in the hospital, when the doctor was talking to him about her mother.

"What are you saying?" he yelled in Italian, then again, "Lila! What are you saying? What are you doing? Tell them it's a mistake. Tell them, Lila!"

Lila was frightened. Her father had never yelled at her before. "Papa," she whispered. She didn't know why everyone was making this fuss over a few words on a piece of paper. She wanted to lie down and put the pillow over her head and not take it off until she knew this time was over.

"Lila! Answer me." Her father had white foamy specks at each side of his mouth. "Why are you telling these lies? Tell them it's a mistake." He stepped across the room, took her by her shoulders, shook her once, hard. "Tell them!" he roared.

The police grabbed Vittorio by the arms, and Lila fell back on the bed. They pulled him away, out of the room, and one of them closed the door again. Lila sat up, and put her hands over her ears, so she couldn't hear her father's voice yelling, and tried to catch her breath. She couldn't seem to breathe properly, she could only take shallow quick breaths that hurt her chest, her throat, her head. Everything hurt.

The young policeman took her next door, to Mrs. Bucci's house. Lila didn't see her father as she left. Mrs. Bucci's house was full; people were sleeping everywhere, even on the couch and the recliner in the living room. Mrs. Bucci shared her bed with her daughter and her daughter's baby; she layered quilts for Lila on the floor beside her bed. All night Lila tossed, slept, woke, dreamed, woke, over and over. Once, in the twilight between consciousness and dreaming, she heard quiet crying. She couldn't be sure if it was her or the baby or Mrs. Bucci's daughter, or all of them.

The next morning a woman came and tried to talk to Lila, but Lila was tired, she didn't understand the questions, didn't want to say anything to make her father mad again. She stared into her lap and wouldn't lift her head until the woman left.

Later the woman came again, carrying a shopping bag full of Lila's clothes. She drove Lila across the city, to some people named Yvonne and Ted.

Ted was hardly ever home, but Yvonne was a big, cheerful woman, always busy, always talking. There were four other children at Ted and Yvonne's; none were their own. Lila slept in a room with two sets of bunkbeds; she had a top bunk, because she was the oldest.

Yvonne left Lila alone. She never asked questions, never made her talk about things Lila couldn't stop thinking about, things that didn't make sense, like her mother dying and her father being so mad at her that she couldn't live with him anymore. When Lila got her first period, Yvonne took her downtown and bought her a bra and a small bottle of Ben Hur cologne.

Lila smiled at everyone. But for a long time she cried at night, with the blanket pulled over her head so the other kids wouldn't hear. She thought about her father, about the way he had yelled at her, the fear and confusion in his voice, the way his lips had trembled. She also thought about the way he smiled at her when she put the supper on the table, the way he smoothed her hair away from her forehead when he came in to say good night. She thought about the picture of her mother on the cabinet in the living room, about her mother's closet, and how she used to go and stand inside it, smelling her mother's smell, after she had died. She thought about her own room, with its pretty wallpaper and matching lampshade.

One night, after two Christmases with Ted and Yvonne, as Lila was falling asleep, she remembered what a girl named Georgia had whispered to her in Gym that afternoon. How Bobby Meyers, a boy in their class, had kissed her on the lips, had tried to put his hand under her sweater. When Lila thought about Bobby kissing Georgia, she realized what had happened. She understood what the words on the note had meant, she knew why Betty Ann had written them. She sat up in the top bunk, her heart pounding, her armpits clammy. She pressed both hands over her mouth and rocked back and forth, back and forth, tears streaming down her face, saying "Papa, Papa," into her hands.

Sitting by the high hospital bed with its raised side, Lila took the thermos and a bowl and spoon from a bag. She filled the bowl and stirred the steaming stew. Only the last few rays of pale autumn daylight came through the loosely woven mesh curtains over the tall window.

Suddenly Vittorio turned his head and opened his eyes. Lila lowered the side bar, smiled at him, and saw his nostrils quiver. She dipped the spoon into the thick meaty sauce, and held it to her father's lips. He hadn't eaten solid food in over two weeks, and she knew that he couldn't digest anything. But still, she kept the spoon there, and without taking his eyes from her face, Vittorio opened his lips and touched his trembling tongue to the sauce. Then he closed his eyes. Lila saw his neck, with its overlapping folds of extra flesh, move, swallowing.

After the taste, Vittorio's mouth rearranged itself into the semblance of a smile.

"Papa?" Lila said. "Can you hear me?"

His small, balding head moved, an almost imperceptible nod.

"I never told you how sorry I am. For what happened, when they took me away." It came out so easily. Lila didn't know why she hadn't been able to say it before, although when she was still young, it seemed to her that it was better to never mention it again, never even think about that terrible time.

Vittorio's eyelids flickered, then lifted. His eyes looked clearer than they had looked in a long time.

"My little Lila," he whispered. "There is no reason to be sorry."

"But I never told you what happened, why it happened, how it was all a stupid mistake. I never even knew what was going on." Her shoulders twitched. "I was so ignorant."

Vittorio's head gave the impression of lifting off the pillow. "Not ignorant. Innocent. Just a child. I blamed only myself." His head fell back, his features slack with the effort.

"Lila," he said, "my beautiful little girl." Then he sighed, a deep sigh, surprisingly loud in the quiet room.

Lila recognized the sigh. It was the sound he had made the night the agency woman had brought her home from Ted and Yvonne's.

Lila and her father had stood in the dim front hall for what seemed like a long time. Lila felt herself getting hotter and hotter in her heavy winter coat, was aware of the water pooling under her boots. She studied the ornate gold leaves on the picture frame behind her father's head. She could feel him looking at her, and she tried to think about something, anything, to keep her face still.

Finally her father had sighed. Just one long, deep sigh. Then he had picked up Lila's hand and pressed it to his cheek. He held her palm against his cheek for perhaps ten seconds, then squeezed it and put it back, by her side.

Tonight, as Vittorio sighed again, Lila realized what the sigh meant. It was not sorrow, disappointment, as she had interpreted it at fourteen, but relief. It's over, the sigh said, it's over, and everything's alright. I love you, you love me, everything's alright.

Lila put the bowl and spoon on the table beside the bed, then leaned forward and put her cheek on her father's hand, lying still and white on the blue hospital blanket. His bones were knobby under the papery flesh. She put her arm up, across his chest, over his frail body.

She stayed like that, her cheek resting lightly on her father's hand, her arm over him, in the darkening room.